THE BEST IS YET TO COME

THE BEST IS YET TO COME

A Short Story Collection: Volume 1

JOHN F. ALLEN

CONTENTS

Publisher's Note:
The Best Is Yet To Come is a work of fiction. All names, characters, and places
are the product of the author's imagination, used in fictitious manner. Any
resemblances to actual persons, places, locales, events, etc. are purely
coincidental.

Rebecca Burton appears courtesy of R.J. Sullivan
The Transit King appears courtesy of E. Chris Garrison

Hydra Publications
Goshen, Kentucky 40026
www.hydrapublications.com

Printed in the United States of America
Second Edition

PUBLISHING CREDITS

"Forest of Shadows" 2013 Originally published in the anthology *Thunder on the Battlefield: Vol I, SWORD*, Seventh Star Press

"HoodRatz" 2013 Originally published in the anthology *In the Bloodstream*, Mocha Memoirs Press

"An Ivory Christmas" 2014 Originally published in the anthology *Gifts of the Magi: A Speculative Holiday Collection*, SFG Publishing

"The Adventures of Star Blazer" 2016 Originally published in the anthology *Trajectories*, Hydra Publications

ACKNOWLEDGMENTS

I would like to use this space to thank God for my gifts and his unconditional love. I'd also like to thank Seventh Star Press, LLC, Mocha Memoirs, Hydra Publications, Stephen Zimmer, Nicole Kurtz, Tony Acree, Dave Creek, R.J. Sullivan, E. Chris Garrison, Jim Powell, Terry Kirts, Sarah Layden, INKlers and the Speculative Fiction Guild. Very special thanks to my editor, Linda Sullivan.

And not to neglect those who have given me continued inspiration to pursue my storyteller's journey, MY FAITHFUL READERS!

This collection is dedicated to my children, Chelcee Shields and Jayden Allen. They taught me to love someone more than life itself, and for that I'm eternally grateful.
Daddy loves you!

FOREWORD BY R.J. SULLIVAN

I'm pleased and honored to write the foreword in this collection, though also a bit intimidated. For many of you readers, this may be your introduction to the imaginative world of John F. Allen, and introducing you to that is quite a task to take on in a few hundred words. John and I have been through a lot together in the last half decade or so, both as storytellers trading and refining ideas, and as independent authors trying to launch our respective careers and take over the world one book at a time. We have bonded like brothers and have frequently feuded in the same manner. But ultimately it is our love and admiration for each other that keep us together on the journey. I think there's a 70s song by Captain and Tenielle that fits here (Google it, kids).

Old songs frequently come up when hanging out with John. Love songs. Dance songs. Great songs of passion. Because if there's one word that I would use to describe John, it's passion. John is passionate about writing, and, as these stories show, he is passionate about life.

He'll discuss with passion the struggles of growing up a black nerd in conservative downtown Indianapolis who preferred watching the Six Million Dollar Man-and reading Star Trek novels over whatever the other kids were doing. Then with the same passion, he'll tell you why Thor could beat Superman in a fight.

That's the John I know. And if you're lucky enough to spend a few minutes to chat with him at a convention or book signing, that's the John you will meet.

But you're not here to read ramblings about the person behind the stories, you want some sort of insight about the stories themselves. The passion I've described above is also the same passion that infuses every one of John's stories and, in my not-so-humble opinion, is ultimately what makes them stand above the pack.

John opens the collection with a slice-of-life low key drama about a little boy named Jared and a misadventure with his big brother Niles in "The Chocolate Malt." As Jared sees and hears things too adult and controversial for his young mind to understand, it's the reader who connects the dots and comes away understanding the implications of what has taken place, and why it's important.

A couple of stories later, you'll come to an early favorite of mine, where you'll meet Jaziri, son of Xiambu, the King of Kimbogo Province. John's warrior prince slays an array of beasts, evil sorcerers, and enemy soldiers as he ventures into the "Forest of Shadows." Jaziri is cut from the same cloth (or is that loincloth?) as the pulp heroes of decades past but presented with a new spin. Jaziri is John's only entry (so far) into the growing genre "Sword and Soul." Hopefully it won't be his last.

You'll then read one of John's more thrilling, chilling tales, and while the title of this collection insists that the best is always "yet to come," I must confess that "HoodRatz" is one of my very favorites. (Shhh. Don't tell him.)

The darker material continues with a holiday twist in "An Ivory Christmas," a story originally published in *Gifts of the Magi*, an anthology co-edited by John, E. Chris Garrison and me. If you're familiar with John's Ivory Blaque novels, you'll love to see the trouble she stumbles upon in this tie-in short story. John even works in an appearance by the always-delightful Transit King (the intellectual property of E. Chris Garrison).

And speaking of tie-ins, pay attention or you might miss a cameo by a character straight out of my own head, Rebecca Burton, who shows up in "The Legend of Machemonedo," a thoroughly enjoyable homage to 80's slasher films, but with a "big" twist.

Just when you think John has plummeted into the dark, he ends the collection on the faster-than-light side, with "The Adventures of Star Blazer," his acclaimed space opera tale every bit as fun as the title promises.

John can write about melancholy childhood with as much passion as he writes about a demon-slaying barbarian. He writes about trauma and ghostly vengeance with the same passion as he writes about a creature attacking teenagers in the woods. He brings that same passion to the story of an assistant on the set of a 50's SF TV show who gets transported to the adventure of a lifetime.

It's John's passion that makes his work so special. And holding on to this passion is why he will deliver on the promise of this title.

The Best is truly Yet to Come. But what we have right now is pretty damn awesome. Enjoy!

R.J. Sullivan
    May 16, 2019
    RJSullivanFiction.com

THE CHOCOLATE MALT

Indianapolis, IN 1975

I t was a bright summer day, although not particularly hot. Jared Alexander had just woken up for the morning to realize that his parents had stepped out and he was left in the care of his older brother, Niles. He knew this because he had peeked out of the side window in his bedroom—which looked over the driveway along the side of the house—and saw that his parents' 1968 Cadillac deVille was missing.

It was a Saturday, so that meant that his parents were probably out running errands. He turned on the small black and white television in his room that looked like a spaceman's helmet. Niles had passed it on to him last Christmas when he'd saved up enough money from his job at an ice cream parlor to buy a bigger color model for himself. Niles had just graduated high school and was going off to college in the fall. Jared couldn't wait to inherit his room, much like Niles had when their older brother Arvin, Jr. had moved out shortly before Jared was born. He had only recently returned from Vietnam and lived with his wife and baby across town.

Super Friends was on and caught Jared's attention for a moment until Aquaman was getting beat up and had to call a whale for help. He turned off the set and sat in front of the window instead.

His bedroom was at the back of the house, and the windows at the rear of the room overlooked the back yard. Some days he would sit for hours observing the family dog, King, a huge German Shepard, and any other animals or neighbors who traveled through the alley behind the house. Jared was a great artist and drew plenty of pictures of the things he'd seen, wherever he happened to be. His mother often referred to it as his "God given talent," although he wasn't exactly sure what that meant.

However, this day as he sat in his bedroom window, he noticed that something had gotten King's attention. He figured it was one of the neighbors who frequently used the alley. Jared found it strange that the dog wasn't barking, as he did when strangers approached. It wasn't until he saw the figure hop the chain link fence and make his way to the side of the house that he realized why King hadn't barked, Joseph Snyder.

Joseph was a friend of Niles who lived up the street. Jared had once heard his father refer to Joseph as "queer." Jared's mother chimed in and explained to him that what his father meant was that Joseph was "unusual." They always argued about Joseph coming over and stormed off to their room to yell. In the evening, whenever they argued, he would sometimes be awakened by what sounded to him like the movement of furniture too heavy to lift, based upon the strained grunts and moaning.

Mr. Alexander was often very hard on Niles and Jared, especially Niles. He encouraged him to go out for sports, but the closest thing to that Niles ever wanted to do was dancing and marching band. Jared could tell that his father wasn't happy with Niles, and it was their mother who took up for him, making their father angry with her, too, just like he knew he'd be angry if he'd caught Joseph sneaking up to their house.

Jared wondered why Joseph had come over when his parents weren't home. He knew that they weren't supposed to have company when his parents weren't home, Niles especially. Although he'd heard his father once say that he'd rather Niles sneak a girl into the house once in a while as opposed to spending so much time with Joseph. He often wondered exactly what it was about Joseph that his father didn't like. At first, Jared had thought that his father didn't like Joseph because he was white, but his mother said that wasn't it. Jared thought Joseph was nice, despite his freakishly long, blond hair and tight colorful clothing. He smiled a lot and seemed to have longer conversations with his mother than anyone, including Niles.

Jared decided to investigate. He tip-toed out of his bedroom and made his way to the back stairs. He sat down on the stairs and slid down one by one to keep them from creaking under his weight. His mother once told him he was the sneakiest child she'd ever seen. He liked to sneak up on her and scare her every chance he got. She told him it was the Indian blood in him, whatever that meant. Doing this was a great source of entertainment for Jared and sent him into a long laughing spell. His mother didn't find it quite as amusing. However, after she stopped yelling at him she'd often join in laughing with him.

Jared listened quietly as he heard Niles and Joseph talking.

"Hey," Niles said.

"Hey, I didn't see your parents' car in the driveway. How long will they be gone?" Joseph asked.

"They just left about five minutes after I called you. I think they won't be back for at least a couple of hours. Jared's here, though. They decided not to take him with them at the last minute."

"Oh, I see. Well, maybe I'll see you another time then," Joseph said.

"Like hell. We had plans for two weeks. I'm not going to let that little shit mess up our plans. Besides he's asleep, which is why they left him here in the first place," Niles said.

Jared continued to listen and wondered why it was so important for Niles and Joseph to be alone together. Most of the time, guys preferred to hang around in groups, although boys Niles age did tend to go on dates with girls. Jared frowned at the thought of being alone with a girl, yuck!

Jared stood by the basement door listening as music started to play. It wasn't the type of music you could dance to—like on Soul Train or American Bandstand—it was slow music like his parents played in their bedroom when they thought he was asleep, and they weren't arguing. Their father had spared no expense in furnishing the second den with the best stereo equipment and largest TV set he could afford.

The stairs leading to the basement were a bit trickier to get down without making noise. But, thanks to the music playing Jared was able to slowly creep down. He saw the bedroom door was shut and quietly tip-toed up to it. Jared stooped down to peer into the keyhole. He couldn't see anything although he heard movement. It sounded to him like they were wrestling. He remembered when his mother had gotten after him and a friend for rough-housing and figured that Niles and Joseph were doing the same.

Jared became bored with listening, so he turned to go back upstairs when he tripped on the stairs. He heard the music stop and he knew he wouldn't have time to make it back upstairs before Niles came out to see what had made the noise. So he stood at the foot of the stairs and waited. Niles came out of the room and stopped short when he saw Jared. His afro was dented, his shirt was un-tucked and his zipper was undone.

"What are you doing down here?" Niles demanded.

"I heard someone come in the house. What are you doing down here?" Jared asked.

"Nothing, just listening to some music is all. You should go back upstairs now."

"Who's in there?" Jared asked. Niles looked like he did when he stayed out too late and got caught by their parents.

"No one."

"Uh-uh, I saw you in there with Joseph. You know you aren't supposed to have company when Mommy and Daddy aren't home. I'm telling," Jared said, as he started up the stairs.

Niles ran to him and grabbed his arm.

"Wait," Niles said. "Joseph thought that Mom and Dad were here when he came by and I told him they were gone so he left."

Jared smirked at Niles and shook his head.

"Let go of me," Jared yelled. "I heard you and Joseph in there wrestling around."

Niles let go of Jared's arm and stared at him with his mouth open.

"What else did you hear," Niles asked. The bedroom door opened, and Jared saw Joseph come out.

"Hey, little guy," Joseph said. He walked slowly towards where Niles and Jared were standing. Joseph smiled at Jared as he always did. Jared noticed that his clothes were in place, unlike Niles. Apparently, Joseph was stronger than he looked, Jared thought.

"Hi," Jared said. He felt a little uneasy with Joseph after this incident, but wondered how important it was to Niles that their parents didn't find out.

"It's okay, I was just leaving. No reason to not be mellow."

Jared looked at him and smiled. "Okay, see you later, Joseph."

Joseph rubbed Jared on the head and walked past him, up the stairs and out the side door. Jared looked at Niles.

"I'm going to my room," Jared said.

"Okay, I'll be up in a minute," Niles said.

A few hours later, Niles was sitting in the living room watching television when Jared came downstairs dressed in a t-shirt, his denim overalls and sneakers. He stood in front of the set and stared at Niles.

"I want a chocolate malt, please," Jared said.

"Okay, when Mom and Dad get home, ask them."

"No, I want it now," Jared said.

"Well, I'm not going to get it for you; we're not supposed to leave the house."

"You weren't supposed to have company, either. Mommy and Daddy might not like it if they found out," Jared said.

"You wouldn't say anything would you, Jared?"

"One chocolate malt, please, or else," Jared said.

Niles glared at him. He got up from the sofa and nudged Jared out of the way before turning off the set.

"Let's go before Mom and Dad get back, you little creep," Niles said.

Jared had insisted that Niles put him in his stroller for the trip to the ice cream parlor. This had proven difficult due to Jared's large size, however.; He didn't care about that; all he wanted was his chocolate malt.

Jared was as happy as a clam; he knew that it was important to Niles that their parents not find out that Joseph had come over while they were away. He also knew that if Niles didn't do what he wanted; he was going to tell on him. Jared was kind of surprised that Niles was so eager to keep him quiet. It wasn't like he hadn't had company over before when he shouldn't have. Usually, Niles was just put on punishment for a couple of weeks and given extra chores, which he didn't like, but soon got over. Only this time, he seemed more worried about their parents finding out. Why? Jared wondered. Maybe it was because he and Joseph had been wrestling when they shouldn't have been.

The ice cream parlor was only four blocks from their house, easily within walking distance. Niles struggled with pushing Jared in the stroller, as he had outgrown it more than a year ago. Their neighborhood was relatively quiet; a mixture of families from various backgrounds. Yet, only a few blocks over, the social climate changed dramatically. There lived the undesirables, which their father often complained about. The ice cream parlor stood as an accepted neutral zone between the blighted area and the nicer area, where Niles and Jared lived.

When they arrived, Niles ordered two large chocolate malts. One of the servers was Joseph—who had recently gotten hired. Jared noticed the odd look that Niles and Joseph gave each other and wondered if they were just happy that he wasn't going to tell their parents. Jared didn't care about Niles and Joseph anymore, now that he had his chocolate malt.

As the cashier was giving Niles his change, three older boys walked into the ice cream parlor. Jared stared at them, because they looked mean. They all wore matching denim jackets with metal studs in the form of a raised fist. The tallest of the three wore a leather hat that snapped in the front. It reminded Jared of the one Rudy wore on Fat Albert.

Niles tried to walk in the opposite direction of the boys and head towards the door. The tall one looked over at Niles and elbowed the others, while laughing and pointing in Niles' direction.

"Hey Sweet-meat, takin' the baby out for a stroll?" the tall mean boy said, snickering.

Niles ignored them and continued for the door. As they were leaving, Jared heard the manager order the boys out of the store. Niles continued on, nearly running from the store. As they rounded the block on their way home, Jared heard shouting and loud laughter from behind them. Niles seemed to walk even faster than before and nearly tipped Jared out of the stroller.

"Look, there's Sugar-pants and his baby," the boys said.

Jared felt a knot in his belly like when he knew he would most likely get a spanking. He didn't like the boys; they sounded mean. He tried to watch what they were doing, but he was scared to look at them.

Niles kept trying to walk past them until the tallest one ran past him and stood in front of the stroller.

"Move out of our way, Sherman," Niles said. His voice was loud but nervous.

"Make me, faggot," Sherman said, grabbing the front of the stroller. Jared started crying. He just wanted to go home. He just wanted to be safe.

Jared watched as Niles came around the front of the stroller, threw his malt in Sherman's face, and then smacked him. He reeled from the blow and grabbed his jaw. Most of the malt had stuck to Sherman's face and hair, while some of it had ran down the front of his clothes.

Jared tried to breathe between sobbing. He tried to avoid looking at the mean boys, but he didn't want to take his eyes off of Niles, because he knew his brother was in trouble.

"You hit me, you cocksucker," Sherman said. He clenched his teeth and looked at Niles with an angry glare. "Get him."

The other two boys grabbed Niles on each side and held

him while Sherman began pummeling him. His eyes went flat; there was no stopping him. Blood spewed from Niles' mouth when Sherman's punch connected. He kept punching Niles in the stomach until he went limp. The other two boys threw Niles to the ground, and then all three took turns kicking him.

Jared covered his face in his hands and continued to cry loudly. He felt scared and helpless. He didn't want his chocolate malt anymore; he just wanted to go home. Jared could feel his body shake in fear and wished he were invisible right then.

When they had finished, each one spat on Niles before running off. A neighbor came out of their house and approached Niles and Jared.

It was sometime later when Jared's parents met them at the hospital. His father was talking to a police officer while his mother sat with him. She held him tight in her arms until he could finally manage to talk.

"It's all my fault," Jared said, as tears ran down his face.

"Honey, it's not your fault. It was those mean boys who beat up your brother," his mother said, hugging him.

"But, if I hadn't asked for a chocolate malt, we would've stayed home," Jared said.

His mother stood as the doctor came out of the emergency room. The doctor told her Niles would make a full recovery, and that they would keep him overnight just to be safe.

"See, baby, your brother's going to be alright."

Jared felt happy that Niles would be okay, but sad because he still felt the knot in his stomach. He hugged his mother tightly and cried quietly against her waist.

. . .

Two days after Niles had come home from the hospital, Jared and his parents went into Niles' bedroom and sat with him. He had just hung up the phone from talking with Arvin, Jr., who was out of town on business, and had called to check up on him, Niles informed them. Jared looked around and noticed the serious looks on everyone's faces, which made him feel anxious. He wondered if what had happened to Niles really was his fault and his parents were about to let him have it.

"Niles, are you okay son?" their father said, as he sat on right side of Nile's bed.

"Yeah, it only hurts when I breathe," Niles said, grinning weakly.

"Jared, are you feeling okay?" Mrs. Alexander asked.

Jared looked sheepishly at her, having always felt she was his greatest ally between his parents. He now wondered if she was so upset that she'd start acting like his father. He looked at Niles, who couldn't seem to look him in the face.

"I guess," Jared said.

"Boys, we want to talk to you about what happened, are you up for it?" their father asked.

Jared nodded his head yes. He was surprised at how calm his father was. It was as though he was just as nervous as I am, Jared thought.

Niles reluctantly nodded, still unable to look at anyone directly.

"How do you feel? Are you still scared?" their mother said. She placed one hand on Niles' hand and the other on Jared's back and gently rubbed it.

Jared shrugged his shoulders and nodded his head yes to his mother's questions. He had a hard time looking at Niles or either of his parents.

"Boys, we need to ask you about what happened," their father said. "Jared, can you be a big boy and talk to us?"

"Don't worry, you won't get into trouble, we promise," their mother said.

Jared looked up into her eyes and immediately felt guilty. He didn't want to tell on Niles, but at the same time, he didn't want to lie to his parents, either. Jared tensed up and felt the knot in his stomach grow tighter by the second. He could feel Niles staring at him, making him even more scared.

"Joseph came over when you were gone. He and Niles were in the basement playing records and I said if he didn't take me to get a chocolate malt, I was gonna tell. I made him take me in my old stroller and that's when the mean boys hurt Niles. I'm sorry. Please, don't be mad at me. I never wanted Niles to be hurt. I'm sorry," Jared said, as he began to cry. The tears stung his eyes. He couldn't take it if his parents blamed him for what happened, even though he blamed himself.

Mr. Alexander looked at Jared in quiet disbelief before he gave Niles a hard stare. Jared shrank back, afraid that his father would start hitting Niles, because Joseph had been over while they were away.

Niles tensed up as though preparing to be hit. He turned his face away from everyone, held a hand up to his face and softly began to cry.

"Shhh…it's okay, honey," their mother said. She hugged both boys in her arms tightly and rocked them slowly. "We aren't mad at either of you; we know what happened wasn't your fault."

Their father sat quietly looking at them. Jared noticed something he'd never seen before; his father had a tear running down his face. He wrapped his arms around Jared, Niles and their mother, holding them tightly. It was the first time they'd all hugged together like that. They all cried together and in that moment there was no guilt, no judgment, only love.

THE SWEETEST AUTUMN

As Sylvia Terrell pulled into the driveway and made her way towards the back of the house, she saw Ronald sitting on the back porch, staring blankly at the ground. A small corner of the sun peaked above the horizon and its faint glow brought little light and no warmth. She lost sight of his dark facial features in the shadows of the dawning day.

She remembered how he used to sit here with her mother and read the Indianapolis Star while sipping hot coffee, with little regard for anyone around him. Now, it seemed to her that sitting on the porch glider had become all he could manage to focus on anymore. She wondered where his mind was and how he'd gotten out of the house without supervision. She'd have to have another discussion with his caregiver, Maria, about locking the upper slides on the doors at night.

The engine rumbled to a stop before the car jerked

forward. Her beat up Honda Accord had seen better days, she thought, as she got out of the car and used her hip to shut the driver's side front door. She made her way from the car to the porch and struggled with the large box containing the last of the pumpkins and apples she needed.

She could hear the porch glider move in an eerie, steady cadence, squeaking from his weight and lack of proper maintenance.

She could have sworn she'd smelled the scent of jasmine on the cold breeze, as the bite of the early autumn air nipped at Sylvia's face. The sweet, airy aroma was odd since the jasmine from the backyard was out of season. Perhaps Maria had been wearing the fragrance again, something Sylvia hated as it brought back painful memories of her late mother.

The cool air permeated her wig and loose-fitting denim jeans. Sylvia was still recovering from the last of her chemo treatments and had been warned to take it easy. She couldn't afford the luxury, not with the money she made from her job at the post office and the expenses of caring for her father.

In the past, she had been at one with the streets, a wild child by anyone's definition, and because of the circumstances stemming from her troubled youth, along with Ronald's own unavailability, she hardly knew him. So, it was odd for her to refer to him as, 'Papi,' like she once had. Sylvia had called him by his given name since she'd left home twenty-four years ago. Somehow, over the course of their relationship, he stopped being her Papi and became Ronald—her mother's husband.

Sylvia shifted the box onto her hip, opened the back door

and called for Maria. Within moments, a short, stocky Latina appeared at the back door. She wore pink hospital scrubs and white sneakers; her jet-black hair was pulled back into a pony-tail, which hung down to her buttocks.

Maria Perez had been Ronald's caregiver for the past year. Sylvia's coworker Elaine—whose brother had been in her care when he had been dying from AIDS—had recommended a nursing agency. The very next day, Maria arrived at their door. Sylvia—almost immediately—didn't take to Maria, but because she was willing to work as a live-in domestic, she was tolerated. There was something about her that irked Sylvia and she couldn't quite put a finger on it.

Maybe it was the jasmine, she thought.

Yet, even the mere sight of her was repulsive, and seeing her with Ronald only added fuel to the fire. But she couldn't deny that Ronald seemed to be infatuated with her, and she knew if she fired her it would upset him. It sometimes sick-ened her the way he responded to Maria, as though she were the only person in the world.

"Why is Ronald out here unsupervised?" Sylvia asked. She noticed Maria's eyes shifted from left to right as she rubbed her hands together. Her reddish-brown complexion turned ashen.

"Mr. Terrell insisted on getting some air, so I put him here on the porch. The phone rang and I forgot to bring the cordless with me," she muttered. Her thick Latino accent made it diffi-cult to understand her words. Maria took the box from Sylvia and headed into the kitchen.

Sylvia had spent so many years wasting her life out in the

streets, getting high and partying from sun up 'til sundown, lying to get what she wanted. She could tell that Maria wasn't being completely honest with her.

Sylvia followed Maria into the kitchen and leaned against the doorframe and watched her as she set the pumpkins and apples out on the kitchen counter.

"Ronald is not to be outside of the house without supervision at any time, is that clear?" Sylvia said. Maria averted her gaze and frowned in silence.

"Yes, Ms. Terrell." Maria said, and shuffled off towards her room.

Sylvia waited until she heard Maria's bedroom door close and walked through the house, into the living room and past the mantle, angry at Maria's negligence. She had made up her mind that this would be the last time she spoke to her about this. The next slip up and she would replace her, no matter how fond Ronald had become of her.

As she fumed, she glanced at the mantle and saw the picture. She could've sworn it had been packed away with her mother's belongings. It was her earliest memory and the only memory she had of her entire family together in one place. She had just turned five and her older brothers, Henry and Paul, were thirteen and seventeen, respectively. They were forced to go to the Indiana State Fair that year, despite the record heat. Her mother had insisted that they go and went so far as to threaten them with extra chores and no dinner if they complained. Ronald had given in to her mother's pleading for a family outing, as though she knew of the tragedies to come.

Katherine had wanted them to be a real family and have a

shared memory of that time. She had been orphaned in her late teens and—like many other Puerto Ricans during the 1950's—migrated to the United States for a better life. A former resident of Humboldt Park in Chicago, she moved to Indiana after meeting—and eventually marrying—Ronald, a young Marine in 1963.

They had all loaded up into the wood paneled station wagon and drove the twenty miles to the fairgrounds. She remembered the wagon as a container of misery which sought to consume them as their bodies stuck to its leather interior. They watched other families drive by with their windows up, in comfort, not a hair out of place. The other children—white ones—would stare at them and make faces. No one seemed to notice but her and her brothers. Their parents acted as though they were in another world altogether, unaffected by the maladies of the kids or even their own. She later learned that for her parents, it was the better part of valor to ignore the gestures of racism.

Despite the heat and the disapproving stares, they'd managed to have a good time. Sylvia's mother was all smiles the entire day. Ronald, who was usually a solitary and detached figure, seemed to have enjoyed himself, laughing and interacting with all of them in ways he rarely did. He'd hoisted Sylvia onto his shoulders and carried her through the crowd when she was too tired to walk. His smile comforted her when she was cranky from having eaten too much. Even Paul and Henry got along without bickering much that day.

She walked to the back door and watched Ronald. The memories recessed to the back of her mind and she focused on the here and now. His shoulders slumped as he pulled the wool shawl tighter around him, as though attempting to gain comfort and protection from the elements. He started to move his fingers on his lap, dialing an invisible phone as he stared at his feet. Sylvia wondered what he was thinking at that moment.

A miasma of dull shapes swirling about the floor of the porch seemed to catch his attention. She watched the movement of them; their colors weren't discernible to her in the pre-dawn light. Some were like teardrops and others like jagged lines. They seemed to have a life of their own as they danced around from here to there, to a random rhythm she couldn't hear.

The sight of him hit her, reminded her of the defeated look he had after the news of Paul's death in a drunk-driving accident. Between her parents, Paul's death seemed to affect her mother the hardest. She often sat quietly in her room, while Sylvia played outside and Henry hung out with his friends at the pool hall, her bright smile and infectious laughter had become practically non-existent.

Ronald had made himself more accessible to Sylvia following Paul's death. At the age of seven—she barely understood much of what was going on at that time—it was of great comfort to have most of her father's attention. They were practically inseparable for a long while afterward. She often attributed her tomboy nature to this time in her life. Even still, she longed for the closeness she'd once shared with her mother.

Not much time had passed before Sylvia's Brother Henry

was convicted of murdering his ex-girlfriend and sentenced to life in prison. Afterwards, Ronald shut out everyone including her and her mother. He immersed himself into his work, taking overtime whenever it was offered. It was after this that she rebelled and took to the streets, where she attempted to escape the tragedies and loneliness of her life.

The next day, when Sylvia arrived home from work, she found Maria in the kitchen prepping Ronald's meals for the following day. Sylvia looked at her with a twinge of bitterness.

Maria smiled at her and kept working silently.

"Where's Ronald," Sylvia asked.

"I put him to bed early," Maria said.

"Why? I thought he was on a schedule."

Maria's shoulders rose and fell. "He was tired, he had a long day."

"Long day, what the hell does that mean," Sylvia turned to face Maria, standing less than two feet away from her.

Maria stopped what she was doing, took a deep breath and locked onto Sylvia with a steady gaze. "He got a little confused and had some outbursts which stressed him out."

Outbursts? What the hell does she mean by that?

"Why didn't you call me? I should've been notified," Sylvia said.

"He's fine, Ms. Terrell, this happens from time to time in people with his condition. If I called you every time it did, you wouldn't be able to work. Besides, it's my job to handle it; it's what I'm paid to do."

Maria took the food she had been prepping and placed it

into the refrigerator. "If that will be all, I will retire to my room." Not waiting for a reply, she turned and walked away.

Sylvia stood there both angry and embarrassed. Every fiber of her being wanted to slap the taste out of Maria's mouth and hurl belittling retorts at her. However, she had made a valid point. Handling things concerning her father was what she was paid for.

But, perhaps that should change, she thought.

Later that night, Sylvia awoke to the sound of a loud crash. She sat up with a start. The light from the harvest moon shined through the slats of her window blind, creating odd patterned bars of light across her bed.

She raced out of her room and down the hall to Ronald's room. The door was opened, and Ronald was gone.

"Ronald," she shouted.

She heard a loud voice coming from downstairs. Sylvia nearly tripped down the stairs as she hurried into the living room.

When she turned the corner, she saw Ronald pointing at the air, yelling at the sofa. Maria rubbed his back and spoke to him in a soothing voice. A shelf of ceramics lay broken on the floor.

"It's okay Ronald, he didn't mean it," Maria said.

"What's going on here," Sylvia said.

"Shhh…" Maria said, as she waved for Sylvia to stay back.

"No, Henry's got to learn that acting out is not accepted. He can't go around bullying folks; it just isn't right. If he doesn't learn to behave, he might end up hurt, in jail or worse," Ronald said.

Sylvia's mouth fell open. She remembered a conversation like that one which took place almost thirty years ago.

"Please Ronald, let's go back to bed," Sylvia said. She walked over to her father and placed her hand on his shoulder.

"Dammit no, Katherine," Ronald said, as he reached back and struck Sylvia.

She fell over an end table and hit the ground hard. She could feel that her cheek had already begun to swell. A tentacle of fear crept its way down her spine. Ronald turned and she saw the fury in his red glaring eyes. As his chest heaved with strained grunts, he scowled at her with a malice she was unaccustomed to.

As Ronald made his way towards Sylvia, Maria stepped between them. She stood still and firm. Sylvia felt the tears as they burned down her cheeks.

"Ronald enough, Henry has learned his lesson. Sylvia didn't mean any harm," Maria said.

Sylvia looked on in awe. As the scent of jasmine filled her nostrils, she could have sworn her mother was standing there. A wave of silky black hair flowed down Maria's back.

Ronald stopped. He looked at Maria as though no one else was in the room. Sylvia noticed the look in his eyes had turned from anger to love.

Maria reached around his waist and guided him to the stairs. Sylvia watched as he calmly walked with her up the stairs, his head held low.

What the hell was that, Sylvia thought.

She could feel the anger surge through her like steam in a boiler.

Who did this bitch think she was?

Fifteen minutes had passed as Sylvia had finally regained enough strength to clean up the shards of broken pottery which littered the floor. As she turned towards the kitchen with a dustpan full of debris in hand, she came up short.

Maria had been standing behind her. Sylvia yelped in surprise and dropped the dustpan and broom.

"Jesus, you scared the shit out of me."

"I'm sorry, Ms. Terrell. I thought that you'd want to know that Ronald is back in his bed asleep now," Maria said.

Sylvia glared at her with a venomous stare.

I bet she couldn't wait to come down here and gloat about how I got slapped around while she was able to calm Ronald down, Sylvia thought.

"What do you want, Maria?"

A wan smile slid across Maria's face.

"Nothing. Why don't you go back to bed, while I get this cleaned up," Maria said, as she reached down for the broom and dustpan.

Sylvia continued to glare at her for a moment before she stepped over the fallen shards of ceramic and went back upstairs in silence.

Later that week, Sylvia had decided to take some vacation days to spend more time with Ronald. Maria had informed Sylvia that since she would be there to take care of Ronald that she wanted to visit family. Before she left, Sylvia told

Maria that she had something she wanted to speak with her about.

"You wanted to speak with me, Ms. Terrell?" Maria took a seat on the sofa across from Sylvia, while Ronald was taking his afternoon nap.

"Yes, I did." Sylvia looked at Maria, with a firm gaze. "I have taken an extended leave of absence from my job and I intend on devoting my time and energies to Ronald's welfare. I am well aware that Ronald has grown very fond of you, and while your work here has been more than adequate, I'm afraid that I'm going to have to let you go."

Maria shifted on the sofa, returning Sylvia's gaze with silent and equal intensity.

"I feel that it is best that you make other living arrangements while you're away. I think this would be in Ronald's best interest, also." Sylvia watched Maria curiously. "I can arrange to have your belongings sent wherever you'd like."

Maria stood up quietly and went to her room.

Sylvia closed her eyes and sighed with relief. Ronald would just have to adjust to life without her. It was for the best, wasn't it, she thought.

Maria returned twenty minutes later with two suit cases. She walked them to the front door and sat them down before turning back to Sylvia, who was still seated where she'd left her.

"A list of everything you'll need is posted on the refrigerator along with a phone number where you can reach me, when you need me. Also, I left my house keys on the key rack by the back door. Please tell Ronald in the kindest way possible," Maria said. She gathered her luggage and left without another word.

Sylvia stared at the front door for a few moments after it closed and assured herself that she had done the right thing. After all, it was about time she took on the responsibility of Ronald for herself.

Sylvia had found a box of index cards amongst the canned goods while organizing the pantry. It contained her mother's recipes for pumpkin pie and homemade apple cider. As a child, she had been a tomboy and never liked playing with dolls or cooking in the kitchen. She'd learned enough to fix breakfast and sandwiches. It was only the year before her mother passed away that she learned to make her autumn favorites.

The kitchen window was opened a crack, allowing the essence of autumn to drift into the house. The scent of wet leaves on the chilly air, mingled with the birch tree in the backyard, a fresh pot of coffee, freshly made apple cider and the pumpkin pies. She smiled as she took one of the pies out of the window sill, where it had been set to cool, thinking of her mother and how much she loved this time of year.

Sylvia cut a slice of pie and put it onto a small plate. The scent of nutmeg wafted into her nostrils, edible aromatherapy. She topped it off with a dollop of whipped cream and set it aside while she poured Ronald a cup of coffee, black with sugar. She thought of how her mother used to do this very same thing for him every year, for as long as she could remember…

That night, Sylvia tossed and turned sleepless in bed.

She opened her eyes with a start to the scent of jasmine. It permeated the air with its sweet and pervasive aroma.

She drew it in.

Again, the scent of jasmine, she thought.

Sylvia sat up and looked to see if she'd left her window open. As she got up to check it, the soft tinkle of wind chimes sounded from the back porch.

Strange, she thought, as the air from the window hung in the breezeless night.

As she gazed past her reflection in the dark glass, she stood there shivering despite the unseasonably warm night.

She watched as a layer of mist rolled around the ground. The haze slowly crept along and billowed like fallen clouds.

The shadows of gnarled tree limbs made grotesque shapes across the backyard shed in the light of the early October moon. The ground was carpeted in dew-soaked leaves between the wisps of trundled vapor.

The creak of the porch glider lifted the hackles of her neck.

Ronald, she thought.

Sylvia made her way down the hall and looked in on Ronald's room. She saw him curled in his bed fast asleep. The light even sound of his breathing was normally comforting, but not so much at that moment.

If Ronald was here asleep, then who was outside on the porch swing, she wondered.

She started to knock on Maria's door, but remembered that she'd fired her earlier that day.

She slowly turned from the closed door, tip-toed down the

stairs and made her way through the kitchen. The back door was slightly ajar. The steady cadence of the porch glider continued, and the wind chimes tinkled even louder.

An icy tendril of fear made its way down her spine. She reached out to the door and slowly pulled it open. Sylvia pushed the screen door open and stopped in the doorway, frozen in place.

A diaphanous, dreamlike figure fused with the rolling fog and swayed on the glider. It was bathed in the pale moonlight and shimmered in an iridescent aura.

It turned and stood. Sylvia was stationary, unable to move or speak. The figure coalesced with the mist and there stood Katherine Terrell.

Sylvia remembered her mother as the bravest woman she'd ever known and every autumn she could especially feel her mother's presence even more greatly than the one before, but never like this.

Her memories of her mother grew sharper during this season more so than any other time of the year. Her mother had taught her how to be a woman without even trying or without Sylvia even realizing she had been listening. It had taken her nearly twenty years to learn those subtle lessons and even then, she had yet to use them for what they were worth.

Ronald thought she didn't know about his illness, so she allowed him to keep his dignity, and to protect her from his own suffering, so that his attention could be focused on her for once.

Her mother's once glowing chestnut colored skin looked dull, like lifeless parchment shrink-wrapped around her thin skeletal frame. It had pained Sylvia to see her mother like that, how she'd looked before she died. She had been powerless to do anything about it. Her sunken eyes were craters of sorrow and regret. In that moment, they spoke of the loss she had endured. Sylvia remembered what reached out to her as her mother had lain before her dying.

"You need your father," Katherine said. Sylvia studied her mother carefully and what had once been a silky waterfall of jet-black hair had turned to strands of white, which framed her gaunt face.

"Mami, why are we talking about Ronald? I need you. I need you to tell me that everything will be okay," Sylvia said.

"Everything will be okay, sweetheart. I know that you're scared. I know that you don't know what to expect, but GOD will provide all that you need and more. Trust Him and trust Him within you. Ronald isn't perfect and neither was I, but one thing we did do was love you kids, and that never changed. After Paul died, we both were lost. Henry was in and out of trouble and you needed more and more of our attention. Ronald never had the opportunity to grieve, because he sacrificed that in order to allow me to do it." Sylvia turned away from Katherine and took a deep breath.

Why couldn't GOD have healed Mama? Why couldn't it have been you instead of her, she thought, looking over at Ronald. She rubbed her face until it was raw, trying to abate the flow of her tears. Sylvia remembered her mother's answer to that very question, the moment after she uttered it.

Sylvia reeled from the blow; her face stung from the force of her mother's hand. Her eyes were wide with disbelief as they welled with tears of pain.

"You need him," Katherine rubbed her hand and sighed. The silence lingered as both women searched for words.

"Sylvia, he is your father and I know that you love him. I know that he hurt you and you hurt him. I need for you to watch after him, he's ill."

"Ill, what do you mean ill?"

"Your father has onset Alzheimer's disease. He doesn't know that I know about it. His forgetfulness and unwillingness to drive much anymore had nothing to do with age," Katherine said.

As the shock of her mother's words hit her, tears rolled down Sylvia's face. She struggled to breathe and swallow as their magnitude became a tangible knot in her throat.

"Promise me that you will watch after him."

"I promise Mami," Sylvia said. She reached out to hug her mother and laid her head on the sick woman's breast. Katherine recited the poem she often repeated to Sylvia when she was a child.

Autumn, sweet autumn/A time for ending/and sowing the seeds/of new beginnings/At the setting of the sun/when my harvest is done/and my labor has taken its toll/I live through the winter/and look forward to spring/when the fruits of my labor unfold/It is then that I sing/my praises to you/O-Sweetest Autumn.

She listened as her mother's heartbeat grew fainter with each passing second and each word she uttered.

· · ·

Sylvia snapped back to the present. At first her breath was caught in her throat, then she was breathing hard as though she'd just run a marathon. As she shivered in the night air, she could see her icy breath flow from her opened mouth.

Katherine's figure slowly walked past Sylvia, and into the distance. A trail of haze followed her like an eerie wedding dress train.

"Mami, where are you going?"

Her mother's form stopped and turned towards Sylvia. A bright smile swooped across her face.

It turned and again walked towards the shed in silence, as it merged with the fog.

That moment when her mother's image evaporated into nothingness, would stay with Sylvia forever.

Late the next afternoon, Sylvia moved in silence. She had long since fed Ronald his dinner and settled him into his favorite chair in the living room.

She went back into the kitchen and brewed a fresh pot of coffee. Sylvia took the pumpkin pie from the refrigerator and set it on the counter. She cut a large slice and placed it on a paper plate.

As she popped her slice of pie in the microwave, she looked out of the window to the back porch and thought of last night. A shiver crawled through her body. Sylvia closed her eyes and took a deep breath. She could smell the fragrance of jasmine again, only this time it mingled with the scent of her warming pie and made for a sweet kaleidoscope of aromas.

Sylvia made her way back to the living room. She held the

coffee mug and plate in her hands, and nearly convulsed, as she glared at Ronald. Her tears felt like molten lava pouring from her eyes. Sylvia looked at the frail husk of a man who sat in the recliner, sleeping. Sylvia set down her mug and plate before she got a blanket out of the closet to cover Ronald up. She sat and watched him sleep while she drank her coffee and ate her pie.

He was no longer the strong, invincible man her mother had fallen in love with, or that she had once considered her hero. That incarnation of him had died years ago, but despite her anger and resentment, he was still her father.

"Why didn't you trust us, Ronald?" she said, as she laid the plate and mug on the end table next to the sofa. "Mami and I could have been there for you, if you'd have let us."

Twenty minutes later, Sylvia took her coffee mug and plate into the kitchen and placed them in the sink. She stood near the refrigerator, and a flash of silver caught her eye as she glanced at the key rack. It reminded her of Maria and how, since she'd left, Ronald hadn't been the same. It was as though a small light had been extinguished from his eyes.

She turned and looked at the schedule Maria had left, and then looked at her watch before she realized it was after six o'clock. It was time for Ronald to wake up and take his meds. She knew if he slept too long, she'd have trouble putting him down for the night.

The sound of faint voices caught her ears. She could have sworn she heard him having a conversation with someone as she entered the living room, but when she looked at him he was asleep in the recliner. Another odd chilliness swept through the room; she shivered.

Damned insulation isn't worth two dead flies, she thought.

"Ronald, it's time to take your meds," Sylvia said, as she shook Ronald awake.

He stirred and looked at her blankly. His face was twisted into a mask of frantic horror.

"Katherine, where are you?" he yelled, looking around the room searching.

Sylvia stood rigid. She wasn't at all sure what to say and or do in that moment. She'd never been home alone with Ronald when he'd had one of his episodes; Maria usually handled this.

"Calm down, Ronald. Mami isn't here."

"I want my Katherine," he insisted.

He frantically reached out for someone who wasn't there. Sylvia's heart sank, as she stepped back and watched him struggle to find her mother.

A loud crash came from the kitchen. Sylvia left Ronald to see what had fallen. The index box of recipes had fallen onto the floor and the cards were scattered everywhere. She reached down to pick them up and noticed the backdoor ajar.

Perhaps that was why she'd been chilled earlier. Once she picked up the index cards, she went over to shut the door and heard a loud thud from the living room.

"Katherine! Don't leave me again, take me with you, please!"

Sylvia gasped at what she witnessed. Her father lay at the center of the room in the fetal position. He was crying hysterically.

She felt the panic flutter in her chest and immediately ran to the kitchen. Sylvia went to call the phone number Maria had left on the refrigerator, but the paper was gone. It must have been blown off from the opened door earlier.

Seconds later, she heard voices from the living room. The familiar scent of jasmine filled the air. When she entered, she saw Ronald back in his recliner and Maria by his side.

"Maria, I was just about to call you."

"I had forgotten to leave my keys when I left, so I returned to leave them in the mailbox when I heard Ronald scream. I decided to let myself in. I apologize," Maria said.

Sylvia could have sworn she'd just seen a set of keys on the key rack in the kitchen. The wave of relief she felt, washed over her. It was a good thing that Maria had happened to come back when she did, after having been unceremoniously terminated. In her haste to rid Ronald and herself of Maria, she had come to understand that she had upset a very delicate balance.

"Katherine," Ronald whispered.

Sylvia looked on as Maria held his hand in a reassuring gesture. A wave of serenity instantly washed over him, a flicker of that missing light returned.

"I'm here, Ronald," Maria said. She lovingly grasped his wrist to check his pulse with one hand while taking a damp rag and stroking his forehead with the other.

"Everything is okay, Ronald, I'm here now," Maria said.

"What are we going to do about Sylvia? Katherine, she's our baby," Ronald pleaded.

Sylvia couldn't breathe. All this time and she never known. Her eyes glazed over, she froze, and dumbfounded as she watched this woman became her mother. Her hair, her eyes, it was like she was watching a scene from the past reenacted. The taste of bile rose up in her throat as the tears burned in her eyes.

"I couldn't bear the thought of losing another child. I loved Paul and it hurt me when he died but Sylvia was our baby. She was our miracle. It was my fault that she became reckless and got into trouble. I know you blamed me for it, but not more than I blamed myself," Ronald babbled.

"Shhh…no, Ronald, it wasn't your fault. I knew you loved Sylvia and I never blamed you. Please believe that God will protect her. I have faith and so do you, even if you think you've forgotten. Sylvia will be just fine, you wait and see," Maria said.

Once Ronald had calmed, Maria stood and turned to Sylvia. "Would it be alright if I stayed with him?"

"Sure," Sylvia said.

"Sylvia," Ronald cried out.

"I'm right here, Papi," she said, as she reached out to hold his hand.

"I'm sorry, baby. I'm sorry I wasn't the father you needed me to be. I'm sorry I let you down," he said. Tears streamed down his dark face and left ashy tracks down his cheeks.

"No, Papi, I'm sorry. I pushed you away and blamed you for my own short comings. I never stopped loving you. I love you, Papi, I love you," Sylvia cried. She rested her head against Ronald's chest and held him tight. He rocked her and stroked her head, just as he had when she was a child.

A week later, Sylvia watched in silence as Ronald was interred into the cold, hard ground next to her mother. The large gravestone had already been engraved with Ronald's date of death. The rain poured from the sky and shrouded her in its bitter chill.

She looked around at the legion of people gathered to pay their final respects. Old friends from his childhood, men and women he'd worked with at the post office—some of whom she worked with now—and even her brother Henry had been allowed to attend. She realized in that moment just how much her father had been loved and admired. She was grateful for their support and for finally finding her inner strength. She could lay his body to rest now, because his spirit lived on in her, and she could claim it, much like she'd claimed her mother's when she passed away.

"Sylvia, I'm here for you if you need me," Elaine said. She'd waited until everyone else had made their way from the grave.

"I appreciate the gesture, Elaine. I never got a chance to thank you for recommending the nursing agency," Sylvia said.

"It's no problem, I'm sorry that they weren't what you were looking for."

Sylvia looked at her friend and felt an icy tendril run along her spine. She had always assumed that Maria had been sent from the agency. "How did you know?"

"A friend said that you'd called and told them not to send anyone. She said you'd found a private caregiver to help you with your Dad," Elaine said.

Sylvia smiled and hugged her friend. "I did. Thanks again."

She watched as Elaine joined her husband at their car and they drove off, the last car to leave. Sylvia thought everyone else had left the cemetery until she felt a presence, like a cold hand on her shoulder.

"I knew you were here. Thank you for waiting until everyone else left," Sylvia said.

Sylvia turned to face Maria and removed her sunglasses. She stared at the woman. Words were useless to her in that moment. Sylvia had learned what she needed to know a week ago.

"Sylvia, I don't need thanks for doing what's right. But I do need you to understand something."

Their breath was visible as they spoke. "From the first time I entered his life, I knew it was his only lifeline. I thought that without that connection you'd have lost him when you most needed each other," Maria said.

Sylvia silently reached out and embraced her.

"Thank you," Sylvia said.

The women held each other for what seemed like a lifetime to Sylvia. She said, "I'm sorry; I never should have fired you in the first place. Ronald needed you, and in fact a part of me needed you, too."

When they separated Maria smiled at Sylvia. She nodded to Sylvia in silent acquiescence before she turned and walked away. Sylvia stood and watched nature's spectacle unfold in the empty cemetery. The leaves were stars which fell to the ground in a swirling kaleidoscope of color, pushed by sturdy winds. She turned seconds later to watch after Maria, but she was gone. There was a brief flicker of light and movement in the corner of her eye. She turned to see her mother's figure again, as it smiled at her.

Sylvia looked away as a gust of wind swept through the

cemetery and created a maelstrom of autumn's confetti. They danced across the ground in gentle vortexes.

The figure was gone.

The chilly air refreshed her, and bittersweet memories slid from the recesses of her mind. She thought of her mother's words and put them in perspective.

It was indeed the Sweetest Autumn.

DEVIL DOG

(ORIGINALLY TITLED, NIGHTS OVER EGYPT)

EGYPT: Near the Libyan and Egyptian border, on the
outskirts of the Siwah Oasis;
2011 May: 2300 (GMT+2)

Lazarus saw his breath in the air as the frigid night temperature formed a coating of frost over his body. To him, the night air proved invigorating, as he had been genetically predisposed to adapt to harsher climates. A light coating of coarse black hair covered his exposed sepia skin to protect him in certain temperatures.

He was relaxed and completely attuned to his surroundings. The quiet indigo sky served as a backdrop to a bright full moon that hung high and bathed the desert in its silvery lunar glow.

Lazarus waited patiently for his target to arrive. His body

was hidden partially within a sand dune, which made him virtually undetectable. He worked for an ultra-secret, UN funded, anti-terrorist organization known as G.E.N.E.S.I.S.— Global Elite Network of Espionage Supernatural Investigations and Surveillance. He had been recruited as a special operative for G.E.N.E.S.I.S. due to his unique physical attributes. He belonged to a group referred to—within the covert community—as Neo-Humans.

Neo-Humans were people born with special abilities such as telepathy, tele-kinesis, or in his case an extraordinary physiology. Lazarus had enhanced strength, superhuman agility, speed and reflexes, along with heightened senses--which made night vision goggles and boom mikes unnecessary--as well as advanced healing. Due to his abilities, he aged extremely slow compared to ordinary humans. He had the appearance of a man in his late-thirties even though his chronological age was over two hundred years old.

He earned his codename, "Devil Dog," because of his spirit animal, also known as a Tasmanian Devil. Lazarus was an anomaly not just because of his amazing genetic attributes, but also because he was the last full blooded, native Tasmanian.

The son of an Aboriginal Chieftain, and a fierce warrior in his own right, Lazarus was protector of his tribe during the Black War—a genocidal conflict between European colonists and indigenous Aboriginals from the island of Tasmania.

Whenever G.E.N.E.S.I.S. became involved in an operation, it usually meant that the terrorist threat had to be either Neo-Human or preternatural in origin. And since either one had been classified by UN officials as above Top Secret, it had to be kept out of the general public's purview.

His mission had been to locate and observe the movement of a Libyan terrorist known simply as Baal. Baal was the generic name given to any deity or human official of Semitic origin by the Semites who worshiped them. It also referred to a powerful demon by Christian mystics. G.E.N.E.S.I.S. had been monitoring Baal's movements for nearly a year with Lazarus as the lead operative.

Baal had been shipping illegal weapons into Egypt to support a radical extremist group which threatened to take advantage of the political unrest going on in that region.

Within an hour of the time predicted, a small caravan of transport vehicles made their way through a narrow sand strip directly below where Lazarus was positioned. The vehicles were marked with the Egyptian flag to grant them unchallenged entry into Egypt.

"Devil Dog to base, the target is in sight and on schedule, over," Lazarus said into the headpiece in his ear.

"Copy that Devil Dog. Hold your position and report any unusual activities."

"Clear, standing by."

Lazarus narrowed his gaze, and studied their movements as the convoy made its way past him out of Libya and into Egypt. According to the most recent intel, the radicals smuggling these weapons into Egypt were remnants of a terrorist cell loyal to Gadhafi, who in an attempt to consolidate the region, joined with Mubarak supporters.

It pained Lazarus to witness such civil unrest in his adopted homeland. During World War II, he had worked with the allies as an undercover operative in Egypt, because his appearance enabled him to blend in with the locals.

Years after the war, he became involved with a Neo-Human group of political activists unhappy with the human government. However, when the group—working with fundamentalist army personnel—helped plan the assassination of President Anwar Sadat, he plotted against them and thwarted their efforts. For several years afterwards, he remained off the grid and lived a nomadic existence.

Lazarus, like the native Egyptian citizens as well as the UN, stood with the rebel forces which called for the recent ousting of Egyptian President Mubarak. While in neighboring country Libya, Gadhafi loyalists saw this as an opportunity to strike back against the UN's decision to conduct a US led airstrike against them two months ago.

Along with some Mubarak supporters, the Gadhafi loyalists had plotted to work with B.A.N.E. (Blackmarket Arms Network Exchange)—an international organization of Black-Market arms and intelligence dealers—to design and distribute arms effective against Neo Humans and preternaturals. B.A.N.E. also worked to create genetically enhanced operatives using Neo-Human DNA to defeat UN forces and control the region. G.E.N.E.S.I.S. believed that Baal may have been a product of such experimentations.

Rumors had been spread that Baal purposefully pitted the region against the UN in an effort to divert attention from the forming of a cartel with anti-American dictators on behalf of B.A.N.E. He planned on creating his own sovereign state with an army reminiscent of the ancient Persian army of Xerxes the

Great, only armed with high tech weapons and superhuman soldiers.

Lazarus spotted a civilian vehicle coming in from the east, headed towards the convoy. He wondered if the people in the vehicle were somehow associated with the convoy or, could it have been a case of being in the wrong place at the wrong time.

The vibrations from the tremors were faint but increased in intensity with every five seconds. He hadn't been made aware of any military or seismic activity in this area.

Lazarus tapped his earpiece. "Devil Dog to base, over,"

"Base here."

"Are there any heavy equipment operations being conducted, or any seismic activity occurring in this region," Lazarus asked.

"No, there's no seismic activity and there's no heavy equipment for at least one hundred clicks from your twenty."

Lazarus frowned. "Copy that. I..."

A dark, massive object fell from the sky and landed on the middle truck in the convoy which exploded into a huge fireball. The sound of the explosion sent shockwaves from its center. The other vehicles skidded and crashed into each other; some careened and turned over on their sides.

Twisted, burning metal littered the path. Bodies and various limbs were scattered amongst the debris. In the center of the carnage Lazarus could see a huge figure in the flames. It appeared to be a humanoid creature at least seven feet tall. Its dark, smooth skin reflected the light from the flames which it appeared to be impervious to. The creature's opaque eyes contained an eerie, translucent glow.

"Devil Dog report!"

Lazarus grimaced, "The convoy is under attack; I repeat the convoy is under attack! I'm going in."

"Negative, you are to maintain position."

Lazarus retorted. "There are civilians down there!"

"You have your orders."

"Screw my orders! I won't stand by while innocents are caught in the crossfire! Court martial me later," Lazarus said, before he clicked off his headpiece.

The pickup truck swerved to avoid the destruction ahead of it and the driver lost control. The vehicle flipped on its roof and skidded to an abrupt stop ten yards from the lead vehicle of the convoy.

Lazarus sprang from the sand dune, tumbled down its side and landed on his feet thirty feet from the melee. He stood frozen in astonishment as he witnessed the creature holding two men, one in each hand. Its hands were nearly enclosed around each man's torso. The creature tossed the men into nearby dunes like ragdolls.

The creature wore only a loincloth, and its wrists and ankles were shackled. Huge, thick chains from its wrist shackles were wound around its massive forearms like huge gauntlets. Its movements were smooth and calculated and contained no rage or malice. His own controlled assertion gave Lazarus a deep twinge of fearful astonishment, a feeling he had not been unaccustomed to.

Six radicals opened fire on the creature, to no effect. In fact, it looked over its shoulder at them and appeared to have smiled as the volley of gunfire pelted it. The creature turned to face them and swept its massive right arm in front of it, knocking the men out of its way as though sweeping crumbs off a kitchen counter. The men were flung about twenty feet into the air and landed at least ten yards away from the creature either dead or unconscious.

Lazarus ran towards the civilians trapped in the overturned pickup truck and pried at the driver's side door. It had been wedged shut so he extended his fingernails into huge claws and dug into the handle and locking mechanism of the door, ripping the outer door panel completely off. He then grabbed the door and tore it off its hinges, flinging it several yards away.

Lazarus swiped the seatbelt of the unconscious driver with his razor-sharp claws, pulled him out of the truck and hoisted him onto his shoulder. He then reached back into the truck's passenger seat and freed the unconscious boy from his seatbelt and pulled him across the seat and out of the vehicle. He ran with the man and boy in half leaps and made it five yards away when the truck burst into flames.

The civilians from the truck were both unconscious, which had been for the better, Lazarus thought. He had difficulty believing what he saw. Whatever this creature turned out to be, G.E.N.E.S.I.S. would want to keep a lid on its existence— if possible.

A tall figure emerged from the rear vehicle of the convoy. Dressed in all black, and despite his dusky complexion the flames from the burning vehicles were reflected off the skin of his bald head. He walked towards the creature unarmed, with his hands held out in front of him; his palms emitted an eerie glow. Pulses of white energy were emitted from his hands and contacted the creature, pushing it back from where it stood.

The creature fell to one knee and used its massive arms to shield it from the man's attack. Suddenly, small cyclonic cones of sand erupted on either side of the creature and slammed into it, covering it in a twenty-foot mound of sand.

Lazarus recognized the man as resembling Baal. Although no clear photos of Baal had ever been produced, he fit the basic physical description which INTERPOL had of him. Given his display of Neo-Human abilities, he was almost certain of the identification. Lazarus had longed for some action however; this had been far more than he had bargained for. He switched his headpiece back on and radioed the base.

"Devil Dog to base, the convoy has been destroyed and I have Baal in my sights. He's engaged with some huge humanoid creature of unknown origin. I'm moving the civilians to safety, over."

"Roger that Devil Dog. Take the civilians and evacuate the area immediately, clear."

"Ten-four, out."

Lazarus carried the two civilians to safety up the dune. He did a quick check and outside of some superficial scrapes and visible bruising, they both appeared to be intact. When he finished checking the boy for serious injuries, the man woke up.

He sat up groggily, and looked at the boy, then back in the direction of the destruction below. He then peered into Lazarus' eyes with an astonished and confused expression. "What is going on? Who are you?" the man asked.

If not for his enhanced hearing, Lazarus wouldn't have heard the man speak over the din of the battle waging fifty yards away.

"I've got to get you both to safety. Who I am isn't important. What is important is that we keep moving," Lazarus yelled.

The man tried to stand. "My children?"

Lazarus grabbed his arm. "I've got your son right here sir. You need to stay down."

The man looked over at his son, and then with a frightened and frustrated gaze he scanned the area, searching for something. A distraught look formed on his face.

"What about my daughter?"

"Daughter? Sir, you and the boy were the only ones in the vehicle."

"My daughter was with us, she rode in the bed of the truck," the man said. The man's stark look of desperation hit Lazarus with a wave of anxious horror. The girl must've been thrown from the truck when it overturned. He looked back and saw a motionless figure about twenty yards from the flaming remains of the truck.

"Stay here with your son, I'll go get her," Lazarus said, as he ran back down the dune towards the fracas.

When he reached the bottom of the dune, he saw the mound which encased the creature burst open and send sand flying in every direction. The creature began to glow with a radiant, bluish tinted energy field and struck out at Baal with a huge length of chain from its right wrist, which wrapped around Baal's throat. He struggled to pull the chain from his neck, which ended his energy assault against the creature.

An energy field enveloped Baal and as he writhed within the constraints of the creature's chains, he appeared to slowly wither. Lazarus realized that the creature was likely killing him, and he had to stop it.

"What's the ETA on support," he yelled, into his headpiece.

"ETA ten minutes out."

"Clear," Lazarus said.

One of his primary objectives is to intervene when any paranormal and/or Neo Human terrorist act occurred. But Lazarus knew in his gut that his first obligation must be to the girl's safety.

He scooped her into his arms and bounded up the dune, away from the fracas. Her father's eyes widened when he saw his daughter. Lazarus laid her out and detected a strong pulse. His enhanced hearing allowed him to detect a steady heartbeat.

Lazarus turned to the man. "She's going to be okay. Stay here until help arrives."

"Thank you for saving the lives of my children. My name is Mustafa Abdul Hakeem, I am forever in your debt," as he extended his hand.

Lazarus nodded and accepted Mustafa's hand. "No debt is owed sir; I was just doing the right thing. Stay here, I'll be back."

He rolled back down the hill towards the battle watched as Baal fought to save his life against the behemoth from the skies.

When he skidded to a stop at the foot of the dune, he stood no more than twenty feet away from the fighting figures whose silhouettes reflected the smoldering flames of the carnage they'd caused.

Lazarus charged at the creature with a guttural roar. The

seven-foot giant ignored his advance and continued to pummel its massive fists into Baal, as his life-force slowly ebbed from him.

He pushed off his left foot and became airborne. The indigo beast pivoted its torso with inhuman speed and swatted him with its open right hand. The impact sent Lazarus flying into the nearby wreckage. The weightless sensation lasted a split second before his bones broke and burning twisted metal shredded his flesh.

The pungent fumes of burning fuel, along with the stench of his own burning flesh and hair assaulted his sensitive olfactory glands. His tattered fatigues shriveled and disintegrated into ash. Jagged bones protruded from his charred skin as the pain ate at him like hundreds of attacking fire ants.

Lazarus remembered the first time he'd been burned alive. He hadn't yet discovered the full extent of his healing abilities and knew death could be imminent. Just like before a chilling sensation moved through him in a wave. His broken bones moved back into place and brittle, blackened skin sloughed off his body to be replaced with new unmarred dermis. New hair inched its way through his reborn flesh, muscles realigned themselves and knit into place.

The sounds of his bones crunching with the effort of restructuring meshed with the crackling of the flames and created a deafening symphony of chaos. As he stumbled out of the putrid pyre his skull throbbed with pain and disorientation. Whatever this creature was, it had to be the most powerful thing Lazarus had ever faced.

Stabbing needles of agony receded only to be replaced by blinding fury. An inner darkness enveloped Lazarus and the primal instincts inherited from his spirit animal kicked in. Savagery burned in his eyes as his body morphed.

Fresh pain pricked his nerves, although this time he welcomed the sensation. Raw, animalistic power surged within him as bones once again realigned beneath violent spasms of twitching muscles. His dusky skin sprouted a fine sheen of course, black fur and his nose and mouth extended into a bestial visage.

The creature maintained his hold on Baal. Lazarus watched the life-force drain from his only lead to discovering the identity of those behind B.A.N.E. He'd spent over a year tracking down leads, and with Baal's death, he would be back to square one. This wouldn't look good in his dossier and the brass at G.E.N.E.S.I.S. would not be pleased.

The radiance from Baal's palms flickered and dimmed as his body twitched one final time before it went limp. The husk that had once been known as Baal fell to the sand. His widened eyes glazed over, and his face froze into a rictus death mask.

The chain unfurled itself from his corpse and rewound around the creature's massive forearm. Its indigo skin emitted a growing, bluish glow as though in killing Baal, it had absorbed his life-force.

Lazarus' teeth slid into fangs and razor-sharp talons burst from his fingertips. With a bestial roar he sprang into a roll behind it and leapt onto the monster's back with inhuman speed. He dug his clawed fingers into its flesh and tore at its neck with his fangs.

The creature's body stiffened and appeared surprised when Lazarus' claws penetrated its thick indigo hide. He continued to attack with inhuman agility and ferocity to evade the creature's powerful grasp.

Despite the creature's enormous bulk and Lazarus' amazing agility, it reached around and plucked him from its back. The creature held Lazarus in its hand and with great force slammed him into the desert floor. It raised its gargantuan foot and slammed it down on Lazarus pinning him in place.

He barely remained conscious. If not for his healing capacity he'd have been out cold. Lazarus looked up at the creature with blurred vision and partial coherence. Blood spurted from his mouth, its metallic flavor mixed with that of the creature's flesh, only served to fuel his rage.

"My name is Epic," the creature said, staring down at Lazarus. "I am the last of my race, a highly advanced species, both genetically and technologically, known as the Titans. It is my mission to seek out and destroy The Progeny, as they destroyed my people and laid waste to my home world."

"Baal," Lazarus groaned. He strained to breathe, and the pressure from Epic's weight proved just enough to keep him from starting to heal.

"Yes, you want to know why I killed him and whether I'm a possible threat to this planet's inhabitants. Well, the simplest answer is I killed him because he is a Progeny, and he deserved his fate. As for the humans, I have no quarrel with them; their race is insignificant to me, as they pose no true threat to my mission. I sense that you yourself are unfortunately a descendant of the Progeny. I have no true quarrel with you either however; be certain to tell your human handlers this, 'Don't stand in my way.' While I have no animosity towards them or the children of the Progeny, I will destroy any who stand in my way."

The roar of several Blackhawk helicopters circled above them. Their lights shined down first on the civilians and then Lazarus and Epic. A barrage of gunfire opened against Epic with no effect. He looked up at the choppers and back down to Lazarus.

"Tell them," Epic said. He lifted his foot from Lazarus, turned and leapt away into the air out of sight. One of the Blackhawks pursued Epic after firing heat seeking rockets at him.

Several ground vehicles arrived carrying G.E.N.E.S.I.S. personnel. An emergency medical team helped all three civilians into a military ambulance as ground troops policed the area in search of any survivors amongst Baal's men.

A tall, portly man walked towards Lazarus, who hadn't moved since Epic left. He peered down at him with hard-set, steel gray eyes set in a stone-chiseled, ruddy complexioned face. He wore desert camouflaged fatigues, with silver eagles on his epaulets.

"Devil Dog, report."

"General Ellington," Lazarus responded. As he continued to gasp for air, he managed a weak salute. "I don't know what it was. But it wasn't from around here, it was extremely powerful and it killed Baal along with the entire convoy."

"I can see that Devil Dog, tell me something I don't know. In the meanwhile, I suggest that you use those special abilities of yours to heal yourself, because I want a full debrief when we return to base. And for God's sake man, put some clothes on. You're a man, not an animal…aren't you? Dismissed," the General said, before Lazarus could respond.

Ellington turned and walked towards the smoldering remains of the convoy. A team of medics made their way to Lazarus and helped him onto a stretcher. He looked back at the carnage and shook his head in disbelief.

THE AFRICAN PRINCESS

K enji Harada stood on the upper balcony of his estate on the grounds of Edo Castle. He watched the sun rise above the horizon of Edo Bay, Japan on an early spring morning. The sky was clear and the goose bumps ran the length of his arms. Birds in nearby trees chattered loudly at the approaching dawn. The cherry blossom trees—called sakura—which surrounded his home, had begun to shed their petals. As they carpeted the ground in shades of pink and white, their sweet fragrance scented the air.

The falling of the sakura petals was very symbolic in Japan, and it was customary during this time of year, for people to gather together—sometimes in public—and reflect upon the fragile beauty of life. Many Japanese people wept at the mere sight of the sakura blossoms falling, so if anyone had seen the single tear fall from Kenji's eye, they would not have suspected the true meaning behind it...

. . .

ONE WEEK AGO...

It was around six in the morning when the Dutch ship arrived in Edo Bay. Large shadows were cast across the pier as it loomed closer to the shore. Its massive sails blocked out the rising sun, leaving only a faint aura surrounding the ship. On the upper deck, a web of rigging was supported by three large masts. Atop the center mast was a large flag bearing three horizontal stripes of orange, white and blue.

Several Dutchmen scurried around the upper deck, tossing lines to the Japanese dock workers on the pier below. Standing on the pier awaiting the ship's arrival, was Kenji Harada, the Shogun's foreign trade ambassador and son of the Shogun's chief official. By Japanese standards, he was a tall man, standing nearly six feet. At twenty years of age, he had yet to shave his crown in the traditional Samurai style. He chose to wear his long, jet black hair tied in the back of his head. Accompanying him were Takeshi Yamamoto, the castle trade official, Sagawa Matsuoka, the dock supervisor and two Edo castle soldiers. All of the men save for Matsuoka were Samurai—the ruling class of Japan. The Samurai were the military officials for the honorable Shogun Yoshiro Kitsumoto, sixth Shogun of the Tokugawa reign and the military ruler of Japan.

Each of the Samurai wore gray kimonos that bore the Shogun's seal—a red dragon within a black circle, on their epaulets and across their backs. The Samurai carried two swords—one a long, curved blade called a katana and the other a shorter version called a wakizashi. The swords were a privilege of their rank, which allowed them to have authority over any who weren't Samurai.

Shortly after the ship's lines were secured to the dock, a dozen Dutchmen lined the deck of the ship while six others extended the ramp. The sky had given way to the sun and brightened to a pale azure. The Samurai watched as the ship's crew glared at them until a loud voice rang out from within the interior of the ship. The crewmen stepped aside from the ramp, cowering at the command.

Kenji and the other men stood watching as a tall Dutchman, with long blond hair strolled arrogantly down the ramp towards them. He wore nearly all black which greatly contrasted with his pale hair and skin. He stopped about three feet in front of Kenji. Matsuoka stepped from behind Kenji and stood off to the side and between them. He bowed to the Dutchman and kept his head down. Matsuoka had dealt with the Dutch for many years and spoke their language, so he would serve as interpreter. He had never seen this foreigner before and realized he was new to the Dutch traders.

"I am Captain Jan Messnick of the ship Octund Star. I'm here on behalf of the Dutch Merchant Trading Company," Messnick said, extending his right hand to Kenji, as Matsuoka translated.

Kenji made direct eye contact with the large foreigner yet made no move to shake his hand. In Japan, personal contact such as shaking hands is not customary and often avoided. He instead stepped back two steps and bowed, never taking his eyes off Messnick.

"I am Kenji Harada, the Shogun's ambassador of foreign trade, pleased to make your acquaintance," he said, before Matsuoka translated.

A shrill scream erupted from aboard the ship. Kenji and

the other Samurai looked up at the ship and saw two Dutch crewmen on each side of a woman yelling and grabbing at her. The woman shouted back in kind, in a language which Kenji thought sounded nothing like Dutch.

"Please accept my most sincere apologies Mr. Harada. It appears that Princess Amatu is having some difficulties with my crew," Messnick said, with a lecherous sneer, as Matsuoka translated.

"Who is that woman and why is she struggling with your men," Kenji asked, as he continued to watch the scene aboard the ship.

"That is Princess Amatu. She's from the Ivory Coast, an area in a distant land called Africa. We traded with some natives who were holding her captive. I liberated her from certain death at their hands. I've since grown quite fond of her and decided that in return for saving her life, she would become my personal slave."

Princess Amatu looked over the side of the ship and immediately made eye contact with Kenji. He felt a shiver in his spine, something he'd never felt before...

"My Lord!"

Kenji slowly returned from his reverie to his bed chamber balcony. He turned to find Kentaku, his faithful retainer, behind him on his knees with his head bowed to the floor.

"My Lord, please forgive my intrusion. Lord Yoshi is here and he awaits your presence in the reception room," Kentaku said.

"Very good, Kentaku-san. Inform Lord Yoshi that I will soon join him."

"Yes, my Lord," Kentaku said, before he bowed and rose to leave Kenji's bedchamber.

Kenji stood there momentarily motionless, wondering what news his father had of the Shogun's decision. His fate was likely sealed and either way he was going to face the outcome with honor.

Twenty minutes passed before Kenji joined his father in the reception room. As Kenji entered the room, Kentaku was pouring Lord Yoshi a cup of tea.

"Good morning father," Kenji said, as he bowed. "What news do you have?"

There was a short silence before Lord Yoshi replied.

"The news I bear is not fortuitous I'm afraid. The Shogun has moved against you my son. You are to appear before his court tomorrow," Lord Yoshi said.

A lump formed in Kenji's throat as he listened intently to his father's words...

As the full moon slid above the horizon, the street crowds thinned. Tradesmen and merchants had closed for business to make way for the revelers in search of the night's pleasures. New Year's celebrations put many of the Shogun's samurai in a festive mood which they sought to satiate in the numerous inns and brothels around the city.

Edo Castle stood as a beacon perched upon its hilltop; a monument to be seen by all and an ever-vigilant sentinel to watch over the city's denizens.

Kenji was seated at his favorite table, nestled in the rear corner of the Purple Lotus, a brothel favored by the Harada Clan for decades. He sat with his chief assistant Yoshi Naka-

mura and Takeshi Yamamoto. He watched as the other samurai frolicked with bar maidens, raised their sake cups and sang songs of glorious battles.

Kenji had been unable to erase the scene aboard the Dutch ship from his mind. The sorrowful eyes of the young woman wouldn't go away. He tried to drown the images out with sake and the pleasures of women—like the one who sat on his lap.

"Harada-san, you look troubled. Let me take your mind off of things," the prostitute said.

He ignored the woman, took the entire bottle of sake to his lips and drained it dry. Yoshi and Takeshi looked over at him.

"What is it Harada-san, you have been moping around all day since the Dutch merchant vessel arrived? We will be rid of them by morning, so why do they concern you?" Yoshi said.

Kenji looked at his friend and lifted the woman off his lap.

"Bring us another round of sake, then take your friends and leave us," he told her.

She looked befuddled but complied in silence.

Kenji waited until the woman had brought them their drinks and left before he addressed his friend.

"I do not care for foreigners, especially the European merchants as I never trusted them. However, this one had a tinge of evil about him," Kenji said.

Takeshi laughed. "Since when have the foreigners ever been trustworthy? Why are you allowing their presence to bother you on such a joyous evening? It is a new year; you should be enjoying your sake and the company of the women you chased away."

"I have never understood why the Shogun allows those

uncivilized brutes upon our shores. The goods in which they trade can be obtained from other vendors in closer lands."

"Yes, but those other vendors are the Chinese. You would only have us trade the company of one dog for another in that case," Yoshi said.

"Better the dogs you know...," Kenji replied.

However, it was one of the Shogun's strictest policies not to interfere in foreign affairs, especially those that do not directly involve Japan. As the Shogun's ambassador, Kenji was expected to carry out this policy with complete and unwavering loyalty. According to Bushido—the Samurai code of honor—one must obey and defend one's Lord until death. A Samurai was never to question, deviate from or disobey his Lord in any way. Any Samurai who did so would be considered dishonorable and be expected to commit seppuku—ritual suicide.

A Samurai's greatest honor was to die in battle serving his Lord and country. Despite the huge personal risk and deviation from the Shogun's policies, Kenji felt compelled to take action on this woman's behalf, he would help her escape from her captor and return to her homeland a free woman...

"Kenji are you listening?"

"Yes, father," Kenji said, snapping back from his memories.

"I used every influence I had with the Shogun, yet he would not change his decision. You are to be stripped of your Samurai rank and be executed. As it is, His Excellency is still under advisement to make an example of you, but as a personal favor to me, he will grant you the option of seppuku."

Kenji took a deep breath and sat up straighter, looking into his father's eyes.

"I accept full responsibility for my actions. It was I who slew Messnick and helped the ebony skinned woman to escape. I humbly apologized for any disgrace I have caused His Excellency, my nation and our family. But know this, if I was presented with the same situation, I would act in the same manner."

"Why, son? What spell has that foreign, demon woman cast on you?" Lord Yoshi spat.

"Silence, I will not have you talk this way about the woman I love!"

Lord Yoshi gazed at him in stunned silence, and then turned away in bitter sorrow. Kenji felt his father may have been proud of him for standing up for his beliefs, and at the same time shamed by the impact his actions had brought upon the name of the Harada Clan...

Kenji left his friends at the brothel and headed back to the Harada Estate. He retired to his bedchamber and waited until Kentaku and his father had fallen asleep before he exited through the back of the estate and into the night. He wore a short, black kimono, pants and light soled, split-toed boots called tabi. He wore black face paint around his eyes and a hooded mask to conceal his identity.

He carried with him an assortment of shuriken, a blow dart gun and his short sword as it was a stealthier weapon than his katana.

There were several of the Shogun's soldiers patrolling the grounds however by sticking to the trees he made his way to the castle's outer wall. The soldier patrolling this area was easily distracted by a shuriken Kenji lofted into the air away from his position. As the soldier turned to investigate the sound, Kenji made his way over the wall and out into the woods surrounding Edo Castle.

He made his way to the pier and peeked from behind a tree; he stood and watched the Dutch ship and its crew. The Shogun afforded a small hut near the dock for Merchants to use while business was conducted. Many merchants chose to use the hut for carnal pleasures with local prostitutes. Since they were not allowed to enter Edo proper, they paid Matsuoka to enter Edo and secure women to pleasure them.

Two Edo soldiers stood watch outside of the hut to ensure that the foreigners didn't venture too far.

Kenji kept to the shadows as he moved silently upon the hut. When he made it to the side of the hut facing the woods, he heard a woman's scream. He recognized the scream as the same one he'd heard on the dock earlier that morning. He took advantage of the opportunity that presented itself when the soldiers were distracted by the scream. He closed behind one and rendered him unconscious with quick, well placed blows to the neck. The other slashed at his midsection with a knife. Kenji's catlike reflexes kept the severity of the cut to a minimum, as he grasped his attacker's extended arm and snapped the joint. Before the soldier could counter or yell out for help, Kenji slid behind him and snapped his neck.

He burst his way into the door of the hut and saw Messnick trying to force himself onto Princess Amatu. Kenji's sense of honor and his contempt for this foreigner boiled over in a *flash. He unsheathed his sword and in one swift stroke decapitated Messnick. Princess Amatu started to scream but stopped. She stared into Kenji's face and her face softened in recognition. He pulled back the hood and their eyes locked. Even amid this chaos, he could no more deny his attraction for Amatu than he could take back severing Messnick's head.*

Kenji stared into her onyx eyes and realized that he would love her. His strong sense of honor and justice was inherent in his actions. He had risked everything in saving the foreign princess from her fate as a slave to the Dutch trader. However, it wasn't until now, as she tended to his wounds that he was drawn to her in a way that had nothing to do with integrity or valor. It was a primal, deep-seated connection which he didn't fully understand. Her eyes, her touch, her smell, were all different from the women he was accustomed to. He saw in that moment, her physical stature, her brashness and fierce warrior mentality—which would normally cause him disdain in another woman—were strangely intoxicating to him in this one.

A bell from the watchtower was sounded and forced them from their momentary enchantment. Kenji took Amatu's hand and led her outside of the hut. He knew that soon more soldiers and dock workers would come and discover what had occurred here.

The next morning four of the Shogun's soldiers stood outside of the Harada Estate, two in front and two in back. They were sent on the Shogun's orders to ensure that Kenji complied with his choice of the seppuku ritual. Lord Yoshi knelt on the floor of the reception room.

The two men locked eyes in silence as Kenji slowly

unsheathed his tanto blade. He held the hilt in both hands with the tip of the blade against his abdomen. Several seconds passed before Kenji pierced himself and twisted the knife with a jagged motion. As blood gushed from his body, father and son kept their eyes locked as a silent tear fell from each of their eyes.

FOREST OF SHADOWS

The sun of the new day began to rise above the snow-covered hillocks. He huddled in his makeshift tent as the wind threatened to douse his campfire. Jaziri, son of Xiambu, the King of Kimbogo Province was wrapped in the hide of the giant grizzly bear he had killed the day before. Its flesh had provided him with sustenance that staved off starvation as he planned his travels to the East.

It was a dangerous time in the Forest of Shadows, even more so than usual. Spring had awakened its sleeping denizens, who focused on satiating their hunger. Just as he sought to survive, the great beasts of the forest had pledged the same goal.

He had been forced to live here all winter, the only place where the King's men feared to follow him. King Arturian of Arsuria was nothing if not superstitious, a trait his men shared much to Jaziri' good fortune. Many of the King's men feared the forest due to the legend of a sorceress Heolstor who they believed lived there. According to legend, she was a powerful practitioner of the Black Arts, and nearly as old as time itself. She was known around the entire continent—even as far as his native lands in Cush—as a powerful witch, and the only one who refused to submit to the King.

Jaziri found it fortuitous that in his time in the forest he hadn't crossed paths with the sorceress whose name was spoken only in hushed tones by the villagers in the inn where he had stayed. Shortly after he arrived in the King's village, the innkeeper's daughter—Rasheeda—had been even more forthcoming about the witch and the other evils of the forest after he had serviced her quite well one night. He deflected her inquiries into his reasons for seeking this information by plea-suring her. She had been so fascinated at the prospect of bedding a Cushite warrior that she'd have likely slit her own father's throat in the night, provided him the deed to the inn and hand over all of her father's gold had he asked for it. It was rare for his clansmen to venture so far north, and the sight of a tall, mahogany skinned warrior enthralled most amorous wenches he'd encountered here.

As he made his way to the Eastern edge of the forest, he saw an odd glimmer in the horizon. Ahead, a small clearing housed a large rock formation. The rocks ranged from the size of Jaziri' fist to huge boulders more than half his height.

He drew his long saber and moved cautiously around the stone edifice. The muscles in his neck tensed like spring steel in anticipation of battle.

The ground began to vibrate with a thunderous sound, and the highest rocks rolled down the pile. A tall emaci-ated figure emerged from the center of the mass as the smell of brimstone and rotten flesh filled the air. The skeletal face glared at him and its eye sockets held an uncanny glow. Its gnarled hand gripped a large broadsword.

Jaziri backed as far as the trees allowed him and watched as the creature slid down the rock pile towards him. It was followed by two more battle ready corpses.

The warrior swore in the tongue of his forefathers, his hazel eyes blazed beneath an outcropping of long, braided locks. His dark face contorted into a scowl with teeth bared.

The animated carcasses moved with the dexterity of living foes. One held a large battleax and the last to emerge from the mound wielded a long spear.

Jaziri backed into a tree so they couldn't surround him and waited for their onslaught. The one with the battleax attacked first, with an overhead swing of its weapon. Panther-like reflexes saved Jaziri' head from being hewn from his shoulders.

He rolled to the side and struck out with almost inhuman savagery at the monster with the spear. The skeletal warrior dodged, but not before its spear was severed in two.

Jaziri leapt at the figure with a bloodthirsty cry and ran it through with his saber. He pulled his weapon free from the corpse and spun to meet the figure with the broadsword with a clang of steel.

His muscles strained under the might of the undead creature. Jaziri found himself pinned against the boulders, with his own blade nearly pressed alongside his throat. He struggled to gain ground with the monster's inhuman strength, but to no avail.

The other creatures closed in on him from the sides. He had a split second to act lest he was doomed.

He crouched to the ground, and with his free hand, grabbed a hand sized rock. With all his might, he smashed the rock into the monster's skull.

It slackened with the impact so that it toppled one of the others behind it. With a panther-like twist and shift of his body, Jaziri attacked.

The monster with the battleax lost its head in one deft stroke. Its body continued to swing the weapon with no determinable aim. Jaziri ducked beneath its powerful arc and split it in two at its waist.

He wheeled to find the creature with the broken spear had lunged at him. Jaziri dove under it, rolled to the side and made a backhand slash. His saber severed the monster's leg, and it fell forward into a tree.

With an overhead arc, Jaziri severed the creature's head and limbs. He turned and was met with a blow that sent him into a nearby boulder. Stunned, he groggily sat up against the tree. The remaining monster climbed the mound of boulders and stood atop it.

The clouds overhead began to swirl in a giant vortex and the ominous din of thunder boomed. The creature raised its broadsword to the open sky and a large bolt of lightning struck the sword and enveloped the creature in an aura of energy.

The ground shook and the monster glowed. The bones of the other creatures were pulled to the one atop the mound and fused with it. It grew in height and girth to form a leviathan.

Jaziri glared in awe at the sight of this behemoth which stood before him. The monster leaped down from the mound and struck out at him, but Jaziri had recovered enough by then to avoid its lumbering attack.

He surmised that the only way to fell the creature was to somehow deal it a mighty blow, something he would be unable to do in direct combat.

With simian agility, Jaziri leapt to the side of the creature, grabbed the battleax of the other and scaled the mound of stones, so that he was momentarily behind it. He threw himself at the monster and landed on its back. It struggled to shake him off but couldn't. Jaziri held onto it with every bit of strength he had.

The monster thrashed about and slammed itself into nearby trees to dislodge Jaziri from his perch. He had spotted a cliff about a hundred paces northwest of their location.

Jaziri struck and tugged the creature to guide it towards the cliff. When they had made it to the crag, he raised the battleax and slammed it into the monster's skull and pushed off its back with his feet.

The creature fell forward and over the cliff. Jaziri peered over the crag and watched as it hit the rocks in the water filled chasm below. It was shattered into pieces from the impact and swept away in the raging current of the river.

Jaziri returned to the mound, grabbed his weapons and hurried eastward. As he continued his journey, he thought back on all his encounters with the strange creatures and demonic monsters in these haunted woods. He had destroyed them all and never took a day for granted, but he often wondered if he'd been better off had he faced down the King's men and died in a blaze of glory, than live with the enchanted horrors that roamed within this forest.

Jaziri had been passing through the kingdom from the south, on his way to the far eastern lands of Hoda and Lapenia. He had wanted a change in scenery from the dry lands of the Cardenac Region—where he had last visited—with its devastating sandstorms and tyrannical lieges, although he missed the broad bottomed wenches who had serviced him while he fought in Shah Rojah-Shadu's army.

It is said that the women of the Far East are even more beautiful than those in the lands he had just left. It was something he had been bound and determined to experience for himself. Although in his heart of hearts he knew of none fairer than those of his village, remembering he was the last of his village filled him with emptiness.

He had needed gold and had hired himself out to King Arturian as a palace guard in exchange for it. His detail had been to protect the King's daughter Laila from any threats made by a rivaling kingdom. Laila was the fairest maiden in the land and the King's enemies coveted her hand in marriage, some willing to kidnap her and force the King into merging his kingdom with theirs. King Arturian believed that Laila was the key to some great prophecy that would unite the kingdom under his rule, and for that divination to take place, she had to remain a virgin until her twentieth winter.

It had come to the warrior's attention that the ritual surrounding the prophecy involved the sacrifice of Laila on her twentieth winter. The Arsurian gods would then be pleased and rain down great fortune upon King Arturian. Jaziri saw the King's motivations as despicable and craven. And he was also not a man to turn down the opportunity to bed a beautiful woman, especially when the deed would possibly save her life. So, when Laila became infatuated with him and pursued him for carnal pleasures, it was his honor bound duty to oblige her. He could still smell the honey-suckle and coconut oils in her fire-red hair, mixed with the scent of her jasmine infused flesh as he pounded her from behind. Her moans stifled only by the goose feather pillows afforded her royalty. She had been a good lay and the satis-faction of taking her maiden-head was particularly satisfying as her father had crossed him on numerous occasions by shorting his pay.

When King Arturian caught him while Laila was servicing his phallic region with kisses in her private chamber, he looked as though he'd likely drop dead on the spot. He had clutched his chest and flailed about, moaning his dead wife's name repeatedly, while vowing to join her in the afterlife. He barely managed to call out to his guards, but it was far too late as Jaziri had made his escape through the chamber window. Despite the twenty cubits drop into the moat below, he had managed to not only survive, but also steal a horse and make his way to the Forest of Shadows.

Now that spring had dawned, he would be free to continue his travels through the forest towards the East. He had waited to travel in the lighter weather as his journey over the Metrophian Mountains would prove perilous enough in fair weather, let alone in the heart of winter. He had very little to carry save his sabers, bow and quiver. The horse he had ridden into the forest now served as the fabric for his tent and food for his first few weeks. He had survived by hunting small winter creatures. As they were few and far in-between, he had lost quite a bit of strength over the last month or so. The bear had provided him with much needed energy to begin the hazardous journey ahead.

After a day's journey, he made his way to the eastern edge of the forest. He came upon a clearing and in the distance stood a large hut. Smoke from a fire billowed from its roof, giving it a serene and majestic appearance. A moderate sized stable stood off to the side of it, from which he could hear the faint neighing of horses inside. He had started to pass it by and make his way out of the forest until he saw a woman exit the front of the hut.

Wrapped in a fur cloak with her head uncovered, she stood in the doorway and looked out into the woods where Jaziri stood watching. Even though he was over 300 paces away and partially hidden by a large tree, her gaze seemed to focus in on him. She dropped the woolen cloak to reveal her naked body.

It was the color of a harvest moon and unblemished, as far as he could tell. Her raven hued hair cascaded down along her shoulders and backside. He became mesmerized, and though he fought to turn and continue his journey, he was beckoned.

She turned to walk back into the hut and left the door open. An invitation if Jaziri had ever seen one. Given the way in which she had delivered it and how long it had been since he'd felt the warmth of a woman's flesh, he was unwilling not to accept it. Besides, the sky was growing dark and he'd have to find shelter somewhere. He stealthily made his way to the hut, observing the ground and surrounding areas. Jaziri had found it strange for a beautiful young woman to live on the edge of a haunted forest alone and suspected there was far more to this alluring female than what met his eyes.

He stood cautiously at the entrance to the hut. He saw her

lying on the floor by a hearth, her body again wrapped in furs. The fire was blazing and provided heat like which he had been unaccustomed to for more than a season. Her almond shaped eyes were like that of a doe, innocent and furtive. Yet he knew that she also radiated a quiet strength and energy he couldn't quite fathom.

"Shut the door, warrior, else the warmth of my womb will surely dissipate," she said.

Jaziri complied and continued to watch her from across the room. The interior of the hut was decorated in various animal hides stretched out and affixed to the walls. Odd symbols had been painted into the fur. Shelves housed an assortment of candles, scrolls and small animal skulls. The floor was covered in fur rugs of various tones of brown and gray.

He knew immediately this woman practiced the Dark Arts, and most likely was the sorceress Heolstor. She had somehow used her magicks to make her appear youthful and tempting.

Jaziri had never bedded a witch before. Although there were plenty to be had in the village where he grew up, they had always made him feel wary. His grandmother—Mpho, the village shaman—had placed protection spells on him since birth. She had also given him an amulet to protect him from evil spirits. Even though he'd witnessed some odd happenstances, he placed little stock in the superstitions of his people. She claimed that one day he'd carry out a great historic act and rid the world of an ancient evil. He had seen the power his foremother had wielded with his own eyes but was hesitant to believe that his destiny would be so great. He lived in the present and carved his own destiny with his wits and the steel he wore at his side.

"Who are you, woman?" Jaziri asked, his hand resting on the hilt of his large curved saber. As she stood and dropped her fur covers, he narrowed his gaze. The flickering light from the fire danced across her flawless skin. Her comely appearance belied a virtuousness that certainly didn't apply to her true nature. The carnal expression in her eyes alone spoke volumes of her intent.

"What is it that you seek warrior?" She stepped slowly towards him.

"I am on a journey to the East. What is it that you offer witch?"

She looked at him with an intent gaze. A sly grin slid across her face as the catch-light in her ebon eyes swayed in unison to the hearth's flames.

"I would think that to be apparent, as it is your desire as well. Does that which you see please you, warrior?"

She reached out to him and began to undress him of his bear fur cloak and woolen pantaloons. He stood before her and it appeared that she savored his magnificent physique. He watched as her gaze moved from his face which was framed in the long braids worn by his people, to his broad shoulders, barrel chest, and thick arms. His skin was the color of birch bark as was the case for most of his clansmen.

The witch slid to her knees and covered his manhood with warm, wet kisses. It awakened quickly as she pleasured him. After a while he backed away from her, scooped her up in his arms and carried her to the pallet of fur near the hearth.

He removed his pants and boots before kneeling over her prone frame. She slid onto her knees, turned her head, looked over her shoulder and smiled. He entered her with a savage abandon and vigorously engaged his hips to her own robust cadence.

After an hour of animalistic pleasuring, she laid next to him purring like a satiated cat. Her leg was draped over him as she nuzzled her face into his shoulder. Her hands stirred his manhood as though tempting it to life. As her hand made its way to his chest, her fingers lingered on the amulet beneath his tunic.

Her body tightened as she ripped at his blouse with taloned fingers to reveal the amulet his grandmother had given him decades ago.

"You are no longer welcomed here, warrior! Leave immediately," she spat, and leapt to her feet.

Jaziri smiled. "So my amulet frightens you does it witch? Why is that?"

"You belong to the Tribe of Atumba, my sworn enemies," she said.

"Yes, that's true, but I am not here seeking to destroy you."

She glared at him with a venomous stare, her face already distorted into a nearly demonic visage. "Why did you spend all winter in my forest warrior if not to slay me?"

Jaziri laughed in a bellowing manner. As he clothed himself leisurely, he shook his head at her. "As I told you witch, I am on a journey to the East. Need I remind you it was you who offered the warmth of your fire and the pleasures of your flesh to me?"

"That was before I knew you to be a son of Atumba."

"What is it that you sought from me truly, witch?"

"I was merely lonely, and you appeared to have a strong back."

"That might have been true, but there is more to this than you are speaking of. The legends throughout the kingdom say that any foolish enough to venture into these woods are seldom ever heard from again, and those who do survive speak of great horrors. It was on my way to this area that I encountered demons and monsters, much like those described by the villagers who fear this place."

"You are tenacious, warrior, I will give you that. You have had your pleasure; now leave this place while you still can."

The witch gestured in a manic manner. Jaziri drew his saber in a swift motion and struck at her. She dissolved into vapor and disappeared. A high-pitched shriek filled the room. He warily turned and made his way to the nearest wall. At least with his back to it, he could see whatever was coming, if it was to be seen at all.

While he was astonished by her transformation, he knew that now was not the time to let it deter him from leaving this place. The amulet he wore would only protect him so much, as he was aware that he would have to fight his way out of this place in order to survive.

He reached down with one hand to retrieve his cloak, bow and quiver. The door of the hut blew open and he was sucked outside into the cold dark night. He landed hard in the thick snow. The sting of the bitter cold powder kept him from losing consciousness. He shook his head to clear his thoughts and regain his focus.

The silvery moon hung in the sky like a judging eye, watching him as he struggled for survival. The wind howled and shrieked in the same manner as the witch had. He got to his feet with saber in hand. The trees which lined the clearing formed a dark and foreboding wall to this wicked arena.

The snow blanketed the ground for as far as he could see and appeared undisturbed save for his own foot impressions. He crouched, prepared to attack whatever made its way to him. In an instant the wind stopped howling and the only sound he heard was his heart thumping in his chest.

In the heat of the moment he hadn't noticed until then that the amulet had heated up and now glowed. Close to burning his flesh, his first thought was to rip it off, but he thought better of it, as that might be precisely what the witch wanted.

Jaziri turned in a tight circle and observed the eerie landscape before him. There was a tinge to the sky which he found difficult to recognize. In an explosion of snow, three forms erupted from the ground and sprang towards him. He made them out as Dire wolves, a species long believed to have died out, yet here they stood, snarling at him as plain as the nose on his face.

A wicked laugh pierced the air and alerted his senses even more. He focused on the six glowing amber eyes that surveyed him. The great beasts' fangs dripped with saliva, and gray and white fur lay thick on their bodies. The fur around their necks reminded him of the giant cats from his native land, and from the distance which they stood, appeared to be the same size.

They circled him and slowly moved closer with each pass. He knew the grim odds of destroying all three, but if he must, he would go out of this world in the same manner he'd arrived, fighting.

He drew the short saber with his left hand and stared the deathly trio in their eyes, prepared for battle.

One of the beasts lunged covered the distance in one leap. Jaziri thrust his saber with the full might of his dark, broad shoulders. The blade sunk into the flesh of the dire wolf and tore through muscle and sinew with astounding veracity.

The creature's blood rained down upon him and covered him in its sticky warmth; a pile of steaming entrails rested at his feet. He turned and stood crouched like a lithe jungle cat. Another wolf leapt upon him and knocked him to the ground.

The long saber flew from his hand, and the massive paws of the beast pinned Jaziri' arms. As amber eyes bored into him, warm spittle dripped from its gaping maw.

The other wolf circled them and growled savagely.

As Jaziri prepared to meet Atumba in the afterlife, the creature which had him pinned stiffened and froze in place before Jaziri even heard the sharp sound of the arrow which penetrated the wolf's skull.

He instinctively pushed forward with his left hand and thrust the short saber into the side of the beasts' massive collar of fur with a satisfying thump.

The wolf fell to the side dead, and he rolled to his feet to face the final beast. The creature looked towards the direction in which the arrow had come.

It looked as though it were going to attack him but thought better of it and backed away. The wolf turned and ran towards the forest and was met in full stride by a shaft identical to the one that killed its pack mate.

The beast lay writhing in the snow flailing in its death dance before it stilled. A long arrow protruded from its breast where the heart laid, a pool of blood spread about the snow beneath it.

Jaziri looked to the tree line and spotted a dark cloaked figure in a hood out in the distance. As he picked up his weapons, the figure approached him, the form drew closer. When it was within fifty paces, he recognized the figure as Laila, the King's daughter.

The full light of the moon accentuated her striking, bountiful figure. Pale, straw colored locks spilled from her face and from inside of her hood. She still held a shaft armed in her bow, prepared to let it fly at a moment's notice.

"Are you hurt, warrior?"

"No, I'm well. What are you doing out here in the dead of night no less?" Jaziri said.

"I was seeking you out. I heard the King's guards as they spoke in the inn. They told tales of running you out of the village with a bounty on your head and into the Forest of Shadows. Given the season, I figured that you'd wait it out and attempt to leave shortly after spring arrived."

"Why are you seeking me out, girl? Are you looking to claim the King's bounty?"

"Nay, I wish to join you on your journey, if you'd allow it."

Her porcelain skin glistened, and her sapphire eyes sparkled in the soft moonlight. He had always found her appealing, but strangely now even more so in the light of the moon. Jaziri had to admit that her skills would prove most useful, considering she'd survived the treacheries of this forest. Her company would also serve to appease his desires until he reached his destination.

The piercing shriek of the witch snapped him back to the

present. He'd almost forgotten about her after he'd vanquished her minions.

He and Laila stood back to back and moved in unison to make a tight circle. They heard an odd drone in the distance. He turned his head as five black, winged figures threatened to block out the moon itself.

Jaziri braced against Laila and waited. As they dived at them and filled the air with a putrid odor of brimstone and rotting flesh, the dark demons produced a blood-curling scream. Their eyes glowed red. Taloned claws swiped at Jaziri and Laila and threatened to slice them to ribbons.

Jaziri swung his saber in a wide arc at the lightning fast creatures, but to no avail. The princess let fly an arrow which struck one of the demon's wings. It howled and crashed into the snow in a large plume.

Another creature knocked Jaziri to the ground and circled back to swoop down upon him. Unhurt, Jaziri braced for the attack.

The demon flew into range, and Jaziri turned to his left side and rolled back with his long saber.

Jaziri struck the creature in the torso. The demon sputtered in the air and flew in a reckless manner. The shrill whine of another arrow cut the air as it found its mark and penetrated the demon's skull.

Jaziri regained his bearings and turned towards Laila in time to see one of the demons grab her and take to the sky. He grabbed his bow and notched an arrow, but he was too slow— one of the demons flew into him and knocked him to the ground.

As he struggled back to his feet, he noticed the creature was the one the princess had injured in its wing. It stood and faced Jaziri with glowing eyes and an eerie hiss. Razor sharp fangs dripped with saliva and snapped at the air as it circled him.

"What manner of devil are you?" Jaziri said. He looked about to see Laila, who struggled in the other creature's grasp. They flew about forty feet in the air and circled the clearing.

The demon he faced shrieked with its head to the sky. The other creatures stopped and turned towards it. Jaziri presumed it somehow had communicated with the others.

Another demon closed in on the one which held Laila and attempted to grasp her legs while the other held her shoulders. Jaziri knew they intended to rip her apart in mid-air, a grizzly fate. He had only seconds to act!

He lunged at the bow and arrow lying nearby in the snow. He grabbed them and rolled away from the wounded demon on the ground.

Coming up into a crouch, he notched the arrow and raised the bow to the sky.

The arrow hit the one which held the girl by the shoulders squarely in the heart. It fluttered and descended toward the ground. It released Laila in mid-air, while the other flew off. He was tossed some distance from where he'd stood and landed in a snow drift.

Even as he lay catching his breath, he knew that, had he not been cushioned by the snow and avoided striking a tree, he'd have died.

He struggled to his knees, but the demon was already upon him. It grabbed him around his neck and held him just above the ground. Its rancid breath would have caused Jaziri to retch had his throat not been closed in the creature's talon grip.

"Son of Atumba," the demon hissed. "You are the last of your clan and my only threat. I fled to the north to escape your clan, that threat ends this night!"

"You speak the truth demon; this does end now."

He grasped the amulet and pressed it into the demon's claw.

The creature howled with pain and dropped Jaziri to the ground.

He felt the ground and searched for his saber.

The demon swung with his claw and avoided contact by an arm's length, felling a small tree. The demon struck at Jaziri in a reckless manner. Given its great size and the proximity of the trees, Jaziri could easily avoid the demon's strikes.

Jaziri pushed off a tree and dove through the demon's legs. The beast slammed its clawed hands into the tree that was behind him and snapped it in two.

As though it were a gift from Atumba himself, Jaziri' hand found his long saber. As the demon was about to strike at him again, he turned onto his back. This time, Jaziri struck with his blade and severed the creature's head in one powerful arc.

Its head bounced off a nearby tree and rolled into the woods. Its body fell, first to its knees, then back on its haunches.

The warrior sprang to his feet to find Laila. There remained one more demon, and, given their ferocity, he feared it had likely killed the girl by now.

He looked out among the snowdrifts. When he reached the

area, he spotted her body, partially covered in snow and lying deathly still.

He surveyed the area, but he saw no sign of the last demon.

Jaziri knelt and brushed the snow from the girl. As he pulled her towards him, he searched for signs of life. When she began to stir, he held her tight in his arms to keep her warm. When she finally came to, he helped her to her feet and guided her to the stable, all the while he scanned for any sign of the demon.

He bolted the doors and tended to the girl. He sat her down on a bundle of hay and covered her with her own cloak. He looked to the back of the stable, grabbed some logs from a pile and arranged them in a steeple formation as his father had taught him when he was a boy. He pulled two pieces of flint from the pouch on his sword belt and used them to build a fire in a pit. After a few moments, the bright orange flames licked at the air and provided reassuring warmth and comfort.

Once they were settled, he looked to Laila. She sat on a bundle of hay; her eyes followed him. She rubbed her left hand and kept it hidden within her cloak.

"Are you well?" he said.

She smiled, "Aye, warrior, I am well. Are you?"

"Yes."

"Do you know where those creatures came from?"

"The witch Heolstor, they belong to her. She has enchanted the entire forest, and this is her stable. She preys on all who travel through these woods, and I was to be her next victim."

"How did you manage to evade her?"

"She fears me because I'm the last son of Atumba."

She looked at Jaziri and pulled the fur cloak closer around her body. He rose and busied himself with fastening saddles on the two mares housed in the stable.

When he finished, he came to sit back near the fire, the girl eyed him warily, her gaze frequently drifting to his chest. He pulled the amulet from his tunic and pulled his fur cloak loosely across his shoulders.

"How did you come to be the last of your village?" the girl said.

Jaziri stared into the fire. It was as though he were far removed from the situation at hand. His mind returned to the time he stood and watched his entire village burn to the ground. His parents, siblings and clansmen lay slaughtered in the streets. Women and children brutally mutilated in a massacre the likes of which he had never experienced.

Jaziri was no stranger to war. His father had been chief of his village and there had been plenty of skirmishes with rival villages in the region for centuries before his birth, but it was nothing like the total devastation of an entire community.

He drew a deep breath and answered in a calm voice, "It is believed that a witch came to our village to obtain the knowledge of our elders in an effort to bolster her power in the dark arts."

"So that is why you ventured into this haunted forest; you seek revenge?"

He regarded her with narrowed eyes and studied her expression with earnest. She smiled, and the catch lights from the fire danced in her eyes.

With one fluid motion, Jaziri drew his saber and slashed

out at her. Unlike the last time, he caught her unaware and connected with her torso. However, her powerful magicks gave her inhuman strength and reflexes, so she wasn't completely eviscerated.

He grabbed a flaming faggot from the fire and flung it towards her. The cloak caught fire. She spun in a circle and ripped it off. As she held her belly with her left hand and a pitchfork with the other, her entrails were partially exposed.

"How did you know warrior? My disguise was flawless."

"Yes, but your knowledge of my intimate conversations with Laila was limited. You asked questions which you already knew the answers to and despite your outward appearance matching hers without err; you cannot change your eyes. Not to mention you favored your right hand, Laila is a southpaw and your left hand bears the impression of my amulet, where it burned the flesh of your pet demon."

"Clever warrior, but it is no matter; even in my weakened state I still have the power to destroy you. This is my forest, my land and when you die nothing can stand against me."

"Yes, all of this is yours, however, I am not. I am the weapon of your destruction."

He moved with the speed of a black jungle cat and attacked with the strength of a river horse. Jaziri tore the amulet from his neck and tossed it at the witch. The amulet grazed her shoulder, and she leapt to avoid its touch. This brought her closer to the warrior, and with one swift stoke of his saber deftly cleaved the witch's head from her shoulders.

Her head bounced on the ground and landed in the fire. A whoosh of flame rose to the ceiling and caught the roof on fire. Jaziri grabbed the two horses housed in the stable, opened the door and led them out.

Once he was several paces from the stable, he turned and watched it collapse on itself. The burgeoning flames spread to the hut and took it as well.

A rustling near the edge of the woods caught his attention. He turned with his long saber in hand.

A lone cloaked figure leaned against a tree. Jaziri recognized Laila immediately. He jogged the horses over to her, tied their reins to a sapling and approached her.

He pulled her upright and steadied her in his arms. "I thought I had lost you."

"Nay, not so easily, I'm afraid. I landed in a tree top, which broke my fall, and I remember coming to only to find an old woman bent over me. She began mumbling in some strange language, and the next thing I remember is waking to the sight of flames in the distance."

"The witch is dead, and so are her demons, I would wager. Come; let us take our leave of this place. It will only be a short time before the King's men pursue us through here. Perhaps they will figure that I perished along with you at the hands of the witch."

"Aye, we can only hope, warrior." She wrapped her arms around him and kissed him deeply. He broke their embrace and helped her to mount one of the mares before he straddled the other. They headed east into the Metrophian Mountain range, in search of whatever adventures found them.

HOODRATZ

Haughville, IN 1979

Chills crept along Charlene's spine.

She slowly opened her eyes and peeked out from beneath her sheets. Shafts of moonlight squeezed through the holes in her blind. The humid night air clung to her skin and caused a layer of sweat to form. The air from the opened window carried the odor of grass and sewage that burned her nostrils with its pungency.

The room sat in silence as casted shadows formed grotesque shapes across her bed. Glowing red numbers from her alarm clock were the only other source of light in the room, 3:16 AM.

Scritch, scritch...

A faint scratching sound came from across the room and

under her bed. *My imagination had gotten the best of me,* she thought.

Scritch, scritch…

There it is again!

Something was watching her.

Charlene scanned the room for the source of her torment. She shrank towards the center of the bed. She trembled with fear, as bright red eyes burned in the shadows like stars in a clear midnight sky.

"What the hell is in here?"

The scarlet orbs stared at her without blinking. The hair on Charlene's hackles raised as tendrils of terror tore through her psyche. She pulled the sheet over her head and curled into a ball. Loud squeaking sounds blended with the scratching and grew louder with each second that passed.

Tiny tugs on the sheet sent a wave of frightful chills down her spine. Her breaths came in short bursts and she squeezed her eyes shut. She hoped that at any minute she would wake from this nightmare. The noises grew louder as the weight of several oblong shapes squirmed over her body in frantic motions. The prodding of tiny clawed feet sent ripples of panic through her mind.

"Get away from me," Charlene screamed.

She kicked and screamed at the sheets to dislodge the intruders.

The room lit up in bright white light.

Startled, she blinked away spots. A familiar voice spoke into the room. "Charlene, what's wrong?" She took in Kevin, who stood by the light switch with a curious look on his face.

The intruders were gone. She glanced out of the corner of her eyes and tried to play it off. "Nothing, go back to bed."

"It didn't sound like nothing with you screaming like that."

She turned to look at her little brother. "Go back to bed, I said."

He looked at her and stuck out his tongue. She threw her pillow at him as he slammed her door.

Mama might bitch at her in the morning, but she left the light on while she tried to go back to sleep. After an hour of trembling beneath the covers, she slipped away into sleep.

———

It was Friday and Charlene decided to go by the park on her way to pick Kevin up and walk him home from school. Her best friend Adele volunteered to bring her nosy ass along, much to her chagrin. When they reached the park, they saw a group of guys playing basketball on the raggedy court.

She knew she had died and gone to heaven the first time she laid eyes on him last year. Chocolate skin, lean muscles and a tight fro, he was a ghetto Adonis. He was tall; broad shouldered and had a wide sexy smile. He reminded her of Teddy Pendergrass...so fine!

The waves of energy he exuded enveloped her as she watched him playing b-ball on the playground at Riverside Park. His shirtless torso glistened with sweat as he leapt back and forth with quick reflexes and excellent coordination. Tight red shorts hugged his sculpted ass like they were painted on. Long muscular legs ended in white knee socks and black Chuck Taylor's.

All the girls she knew wanted to be with him, but so far he hadn't claimed any of them. *Why would it be any different for me?* she thought.

All Charlene knew is that she thought he was cute. She was still a virgin unlike the other girls she knew, but if she were gonna give up her Kit Kat to anyone, she wanted it to be him. She just wasn't sure she was ready yet.

Charlene often liked to spend the summer checking out the hot guys playing basketball at the park. Ever since she graduated last year, she spent most of her free time—what little she had—away from home. She spent so much time looking after her little brother Kevin that she sometimes felt like she'd been the one who gave birth to him. At ten, he was far from a baby, but he was too young to really take care of himself. Momma felt that he was impressionable and feared that the streets would claim him, much like they did their father shortly after Kevin's birth.

"Girl, are you listenin' to me?" Adele snapped Charlene out of her fantasy.

"Yeah, sure," Charlene stammered.

"Liar! You all up in La La Land daydreamin' about Tyrese. I don't even see why you wastin' your time on him. He ain't nothin' but trouble."

I'm sure he is, Charlene thought. *Just the kinda trouble I want to get into.*

"How would you know?"

"You know he's the leader of that gang called The Hood-Ratz. They say that Marcy Evans was last seen with him before she disappeared last year," Adele said.

"Please, that heifa was strung out and ran away from her

ho ass mama and drunk ass father. She's probably in Chicago somewhere suckin' dicks and getting high."

"Naw, I don't think so. My cousin Erica and her were friends and she said that Marcy planned to leave, but she was headed down to Kentucky to go to college."

"Just because she went off and left doesn't mean that Tyrese was the reason," Charlene said.

"Well it don't matter much anyway because he ain't studdin' you anyhow."

As Charlene decided she'd had enough of listening to Adele talkin' out the side of her neck, she glanced back at the court and caught Tyrese looking at her. His deep set, espresso eyes bore into her. A shudder traveled down her spine and sent tendrils of electricity through her body. Hot air gushed over her like an oven. Tiny pinpricks nipped at her nerve endings.

His gaze held her, gave her roots and drowned out everything and everyone else. The basketball had been passed and was headed straight for his head, but in one deft motion, he caught it in one hand.

It was damnedest thing Charlene had ever seen.

He tossed the ball back to the other players and walked towards her. She could smell almonds and brown sugar, as though the scent materialized from nowhere. A sly grin spread across his face as he kept moving in her direction. Although she had been captured by his eyes, she couldn't help but notice the swagger in his stride. His thick manhood bounced with every step like a snake in thrall of a charmer.

"Yo, Tyrese, you gonna play ball or what?" a large, bearish looking guy barked.

Tyrese turned his head and cut the other man a narrow eyed glance.

"I better get back to the game, I'll catch you later," he said with a grin.

Gooseflesh covered Charlene's entire body. She didn't care what Adele said, she had already been seeing him secretly for months and tonight might be the night that he made her his woman.

———

The evening started out like any other. Charlene had fixed dinner while her mother slept. She'd fed her little brother, helped him with his homework, and went to her room to listen to the radio in solitude. Her mother worked the graveyard shift at Wishard Hospital, sometimes taking extra shifts just to make ends meet. She hated that her mother was hardly home, and often times she was saddled with the responsibility of caring for Kevin.

Charlene yearned for more out of life than being single, saddled with two kids and barely surviving at a dead-end job. Her father had left them soon after Kevin was born and none of them had heard anything from him since. There had been plenty of ignorant ass Negroes sniffin' around her mama over the years, but none of them wanted to stick around and help raise some other dude's kids.

She had always known that she wanted more out of life. Charlene always dreamed of the glamorous life like the white folks on Dynasty.

Her thoughts immediately turned to Tyrese. Tall, handsome, and he got money. She knew that slinging rock was very different than drilling for oil, but this was still the hood...you did what you had to do to survive!

It was about six o'clock when she heard her mother stirring around in the kitchen. Usually she didn't get up until around ten. Charlene wasn't sleepy yet and it was Friday night, so she decided to take the opportunity find out why her mother was up so early. Charlene stood in the doorway and watched as her mother set the coffee maker to brew before she dug around in the refrigerator to put together some food to take to work.

She wore a torn housecoat, and her large afro sprawled atop her head resembled a used *Brillo* pad. Charlene loved and admired her mother, even though she didn't envy her lot in life. She knew that she was a strong woman to deal with the hand she had been dealt and continue to keep her faith.

"Are you just gonna stand there and stare at me, or are you gonna say somethin'?"

Charlene smiled. She swore that this woman had eyes in the back of her head. "Hey, Mama."

Her mother continued to move about the kitchen with a purpose borne of habit. Once she had set all the food she needed on the counter, she paused to turn towards Charlene. Black circles masked her eyes as red veins threatened to replace the whites. Her haggard expression and slumped posture aside, she was still an attractive woman, another thing that Charlene admired about her.

"What do you want?"

"I heard you up and wanted to see what was going on," she said.

"I'm going in early to pick up a few extra hours before I start my double shift. Kevin is going to spend the night over at the neighbor boy's house tonight."

"Oh…" Charlene said.

She gave her a stern look and pursed her lips. "You thinkin' about going out to see that boy, ain't you?"

Charlene's mouth opened slightly, but she was unable to speak. Her mind raced to counter her mother's question.

"You don't have to say a word. I already know."

Charlene let an uneasy smile spread across her face. "What exactly do you know, Mama?"

"I know you went by the park on your way home from school and talked to that fool, even though I told you to stay away from him."

The weight of her mother's words lingered in the air as she hung her head low.

This woman is always up in my business, she thought. *Then again, it was probably Adele's ass that told her.*

"I don't work a shitty ass job to send you to school and save up money for you to take night classes after you graduate for you to be following up after some knucklehead-ass drug dealer. You gonna fool around and end up knocked up and he ain't gonna be nowhere around to help your ass," her mother said.

"Like mother, like daughter," Charlene said, a split second before her mother's hand lashed out and struck her across the face.

The stinging of her cheeks registered in her mind. Anger welled up inside of her as she glanced in her mother's direction.

"You best watch your mouth, little girl! I tell you what, you want to go chasin' that no good Negro, then go right ahead, but don't think I'll be bending over backwards to help you deal with the mess you make of your life."

Charlene stood in silence and gritted her teeth. "Yes, Ma'am."

She turned to continue getting her food ready for work.

Charlene went back to her room and knew without a doubt that she had to get the hell out of there. She waited an hour after she heard her mother leave and called Tyrese.

———

Charlene had been sneaking out every weekend when her mother worked double shifts to meet with Tyrese. Sometimes they walked around The Circle downtown and held hands. Other times, they would spend hours in his ride smoking weed, drinking Colt 45, making out, or, on a good night, all three. He had been patient and never forced himself on her. He had stopped when she asked, but he was also very possessive of her. He wanted to know where she was and who she was always with.

She didn't like his attitude in that regard, but because he had been so patient and because he was so fine, she put up with it. He never laid his hands on her, but she saw him beat the shit outta some guy who cat called her downtown once. It was exciting that a man would fight over her, but scary that she had to beg him not to kill the guy.

Tyrese decided he wanted them to stay in that night. They smoked a couple joints and drank malt liquor until she felt herself become giddy. Smoke and liquid courage dropped her inhibitions.

"So, what are we going to do tonight?" she asked. A sly smile spread across her face and she giggled.

Tyrese flashed an impish grin. "I've got something to show you."

He led her to his bedroom and shut the door behind them. She sat on the bed and kicked off her boots. The room was large and dark except for an orange lava lamp.

"Let me turn on a brighter light," Charlene said, as she reached for a lamp on the nightstand.

Tyrese quickly reached out and grabbed her wrist. "No, I like it like this."

"Let go of me, you're hurting me," Charlene said.

Charlene didn't imagine her first time going down like this. She wanted Tyrese to be gentle and understanding. She thought she was ready but being manhandled was not sexy.

"Shut the hell up! How long did you think I was gonna keep giving you free weed and beer, without getting something in return? I own theses streets and tonight I own your ass!"

She struggled as he grabbed her other wrist and pushed her down on the bed. His breath smelled of weed and malt liquor, and he forced his mouth over hers. Charlene squirmed and kicked; her breaths were shallow. She tried to scream, but couldn't, because he viciously gnawed at her mouth.

In her high, she was disoriented and weak. She wanted to fight back harder but couldn't. His weight pinned her down and she could feel his hardness against her. She had wanted him to fuck her, but not like this. All her lust for him died in that moment, only to be replaced by revulsion and terror.

"Tyrese," a gravelly voice said.

Its echo dripped with terror and stopped him in his tracks.

They both turned to see a young woman—not much older than Charlene—standing naked in the corner of the room. Her skin was sienna brown and her hair was a large afro.

"Who the fuck are you?" Tyrese demanded. He spun away from Charlene to face the other woman.

Her eyes glowed crimson and a cursory grin revealed large central incisors.

She chuckled.

"Don't act like you don't know me," she said. She stepped forward and further into the dim light from the lava lamp.

"Marcy," he stammered.

"Live and in living color."

"But you're…"

"Dead? Is that the word you're looking for?" she said, with a dark grin.

Charlene's high began to fade as she began to realize what she was seeing. She sat in stunned silence, unable to move or speak.

Tyrese took a step back and reached into his back pocket. He clicked the switchblade into place and dropped into a fighting stance with his arms out in front of him.

"Stay back, bitch, or I'll cut you."

Marcy closed her eyes and emitted a loud and bellowing laugh. "Fool, I don't think so."

Tyrese lunged at her with the knife, and in a blur, Marcy

grabbed his wrist and twisted it. He screamed in agony. An odd lump formed in his forearm and bone pierced the skin.

Charlene shrank against the headboard and cried. She had folded her knees to her chest and wrapped her arms around them. Marcy looked in her direction.

"What do you think I should do to him, sister? Should I tear him limb from limb, or…?" Marcy grabbed his testicles with her free hand and squeezed them. Tyrese attempted to scream, but it came out as whiny groan.

"…should I rip off his balls and force him to eat them?"

Charlene watched in wide eyed horror. The faint sounds of scratching caught her ears.

Scritch, scritch…

It was the same sound she had heard in her dream last night.

Scritch, scritch…

Like soldiers marching in cadence, an army of large, elongated ovoid shapes appeared from the recesses of the room. Glowing red eyes burned in the darkness and stared at Marcy.

"Perhaps we should make him suffer? A quick death is much too kind," Marcy said.

She released Tyrese's arm and he slid into a crumpled mass on the floor.

Tyrese turned towards Charlene. "Help me," he squeaked.

She averted her eyes and buried her face into her knees. A cold shiver of fear crept along her spine and made her body a sheet of gooseflesh.

"Don't hide, you'll miss the best part," Marcy chimed.

Charlene kept her face hidden until her head was snapped

back. Marcy had closed the distance between them and stared at her with eyes like fiery red orbs. "Look," she spat.

The ovoid shapes skittered around Tyrese and surrounded him. Wicked crimson stares bore into him as long tails curled around their forms. The energy in the room amped up as Marcy looked towards them.

They converged on him in a synchronized swarm. Tyrese screamed and writhed as the horde of rodents savagely gnawed at his flesh. Charlene wanted to turn away, but fear of Marcy and the surreal scene itself kept her eyes frozen in place.

A mass of rats covered his body so that only his hands could be seen. He attempted to grasp the vermin and fling them away, but for each one he dislodged, three more appeared. His blood curdling scream slowly turned into muted mewling and pleas for God to help him.

Hot tears stung Charlene's eyes, while his long arms came to rest on the floor and be engulfed within the squirming mass of rats. She trembled in terror and her entire body was covered in a sheet of sweat. In minutes that seemed to stretch out for hours, the rodents slow slid away from their meal. Only the wet skeletal frame of Tyrese remained.

Marcy let go of her hair and walked towards the corpse sprawled akimbo on the floor. She kneeled. Her gaze traveled from head to toe. A grin spread across her brown face and further revealed her elongated front teeth.

"A fitting conclusion, wouldn't you agree?"

Charlene looked at Marcy with wide eyed terror.

"You have absolutely nothing to fear from me, sister. We

were both seduced by this asshole's charm and victims of his wickedness," Marcy said.

"What happened to you?" Charlene managed.

Marcy smiled and stood to her full height. She kicked the skeleton in front of her, made her way to the bed, and sat down next to Charlene.

She glanced in the direction of Tyrese's corpse. "That mutha fucka kidnapped me, viciously raped me and then left me for dead on the outskirts of town. I was found by an old lady from Haiti named Mama Marinette. She pulled me back from the brink of death and infused me with the power to no longer be a victim."

Tiny pinpricks of hot needles pierced the flesh of Charlene's body. A wave of hot energy washed over her and threatened to suffocate her in its intensity. Marcy's eyes grew larger and glowed brighter. A fine sheen of brownish-gray fur sprouted from her soft brown skin.

"You see, Mama Marinette is what the followers of voodoo call a loa—a spirit god. She is very powerful, and she is very protective of her pack. We are kindred souls, you and I. Once you've become one of us and tasted the power of our queen, you'll never be a victim of a man's abuse ever again."

Charlene allowed herself to look up at Marcy. She was caught in the radiant glow of her eyes and found she could not move her body. A blur of movement, and Marcy began gnawing at Charlene's neck. Her consciousness slipped away, and the room faded to black.

AN IVORY CHRISTMAS

Ho, ho, ho my ass!

The holidays have turned from the time of family gatherings and thanksgiving for our blessings into a series of corporate schemes designed to enslave the consumer. And, just like every other good little shopper, I'm out on a Friday evening in the middle of freezing temps and knee high snow, looking for the perfect gifts.

This Christmas was my first as the new and improved Ivory Blaque, mild mannered art gallery owner and art recovery agent by day, immortal magistrate of rogue preternaturals in the Windy City by night. It was also the first time in almost a decade that I had a significant other to shop for.

What to buy your lycan boyfriend, who also happens to be the Alpha of the Chicagoland Pack? I'd initially come up with the idea of a leather collar, chains and a personalized chew toy, but on second thought I realized that might be offensive, despite how much fun the images in my head seemed.

They say it's the most wonderful time of the year and that it brings out the best in everyone. But I've worked in retail, and I'm here to tell you that none of that shit is true. Well, at least not for everyone.

News reports swirled through the area about the mysterious disappearances of children in the greater Chicagoland area, particularly in Lincoln Square—a predominately German neighborhood. When I thought about what those parents were going through, my surly frustrations paled in comparison.

I wasn't strolling down the sidewalk in this 'burg because they had the best bargains. The UN sponsored, clandestine international organization I worked for was called G.E.N.E.S.I.S.—Global Elite Network of Espionage Supernatural Investigations and Surveillance. Director Elijah Bishop, my G.E.N.E.S.I.S. handler, wanted me to snoop around and rule out that these disappearances may be preternatural in nature.

Almost two thirds of the missing person's cases in this country are a result of rogue preternaturals--a disheartening fact--but for this very reason, those cases are left unsolved. I do what I can, but since preternaturals tend to devour any and all evidence of their crimes, tracking them down is challenging, to say the least.

The wind whipped at me like frosty cat-o-nine tails. I wasn't affected by it as much as I would've been prior to my rebirth as an immortal. To keep up appearances, I wore a long dark red, hooded down coat over a festive red, white and green sweater decorated with little elves. A dark red beret, black jeans and knee-high snow boots completed my holiday ensemble.

Thanks to Papa, I inherited a rare genetic trait from a race of inter-dimensional beings known as the Progeny. Long story short, I was no longer entirely human and I possessed strange powers and abilities far beyond those of mortal men.

Of course, I was already light years ahead of mortal men, I am a woman, after all.

As I made my way down the snow-packed sidewalks, I peeked into the storefront windows of every building I passed. Large signs announced sales and discounts that promised to make anyone thrifty enough to take advantage, a smart and valued customer…yeah right!

The cacophonous din of cars, shoppers and the jingling of bells from Salvation Army Santas assaulted my ears from every direction. Groups of shoppers huddled together, shrouded in the mists from their chilled breaths and walked briskly to and fro. Several homeless people gathered around fiery barrels of burning refuge to keep warm. Scenes such as those forced me to reevaluate my Christmas cynicism and pause to take stock in all that I had to be grateful for.

Not everyone owned a successful business which afforded them wealth and status within the community. And then there were those not fortunate enough to have found a significant other to share their life and good fortunes with.

Before I got carried away in my George Bailey moment, a cry rose above the other sounds of the season. A woman screamed; "Help, my baby is missing! Someone please help me."

I spotted a group of people at the end of the block and made my way towards them. The woman's cries were interspersed with sobs. When I finally slipped my way through the crowd, I saw her. She was slender with pale skin and flaxen hair. Large green eyes were wet with tears and puffy eyelids attempted to encase them at irregular intervals.

I placed my hand on her shoulder. She trembled and I assumed it wasn't all from the cold. "Can you tell me what happened?"

The woman sniffled and tried to regain her composure. After a few moments, she spoke in a strained voice. "He took my baby."

"Who took your baby?" I asked.

She stifled a sob. "A man…no, a monster dressed in a Santa Claus suit. He ran by and snatched her into a bag and ran down the alley."

The crowd surrounding us looked on with a mix of disbelief and brusque dismissal. They probably thought she was mentally disturbed or on drugs, but I had a sneaking suspicion she was telling the truth. Bishop had been on the money to send me here.

Over the past twelve years, I'd been one of a few humans to interact in the preternatural world and experience firsthand the brand of evil some of them were capable of. Of course, the faint displaced odor of brimstone and cloven-hooved footprints in the snow also supported her story.

I gently turned her around to face me. "How long ago was your daughter taken?"

"Only a few minutes ago. Please, you've got to help me get my daughter back!"

I nodded. "Stay here and I'll go see if I can find her, they can't have gotten too far." I looked around at the few people still lingering. "Someone call the cops. Ask for Detective Jazz Fitzgerald."

A short, rotund, pale complexioned man dressed in a white, puffed up down coat and a matching watch cap waved his cell phone at me. "I got you covered, lady," he said.

Thanks Michelin Man, I thought as I waved back.

I headed down the dark and desolate alleyway. When I got about halfway down, I drew the God Killers from their holster. I'd inherited the mystical pistols by default when I was hired to retrieve them earlier this year. Bishop had hired me—under false pretenses—and later deemed me the worthy custodian for them. It didn't hurt that I'd bonded with them, either.

From what I knew, they never ran out of ammo and could kill any preternatural creature with a shot to the brain or heart. They could also morph between pistols or swords with a mere thought. I had to admit they were pretty handy tools to have in my line of work. I decided to keep the weapons in their default, pistol-mode. At least until I know what I was dealing with.

I tried my best to keep my boots from crunching the snow, but I knew that there were a dozen different ways a preternatural could detect my presence. The farther in I walked, the darker it got. Luckily, I had better-than-human eyesight, but even that had its limits.

The odor of brimstone intensified, and I heard the faint sound of metal scraping together. I stood about fifty feet from the end of the alley, which ended in a sharp right. Using a dumpster for cover, I slowly peeped around to see what lie ahead.

A shorter corridor ended in a loading dock to what

appeared to be an abandoned building. I approached an opened door next to the dock and entered. The odor of brimstone burned my nostrils and the back of my throat.

Welcome to Hell, I thought.

I stepped inside the pitch-black warehouse, but luckily my senses were several times sharper than an average human's. While I didn't have cat-vision, my eyes adjusted to darkness quickly and allowed me to see things others wouldn't.

I strained in the deafening silence to hear even the slightest sound.

As I made my way to the center of the warehouse floor, a faint whimpering sounded above me. I looked up and barely made out a small figure, which hung upside down from the thirty-foot-high ceiling. It wriggled against the chains that bound it.

It was the girl, I knew it. I turned and slowly scanned the perimeter of the room, pistols steadied in front of me. I saw no sign of the monster; only its foul scent lingered in the air.

The crash of shattered glass broke the silence. Shards fell to the floor in front of me in a jagged shower. A hulking silhouette fell from the skylight and landed atop the fallen glass.

Even in the virtual darkness, the beast stood at least seven feet, dressed in a dingy Santa coat and matching hat. Two large horns protruded from its forehead and curved towards the back of its head to form an omega symbol.

A blood curdling roar pierced the silence and reverberated throughout the mostly empty warehouse floor. The creature bared a maw full of long fangs with ropes of saliva strung between them. Spittle showered me over the distance…yuck!

Not one to ask questions, I fired on the creature. Despite its massiveness, it leapt from my line of fire and used a crate for cover. I kept moving in a counter clockwise circle and continued to fire. I hoped that one of my shots would penetrate the crate and land in a kill zone.

My mystical pistols could kill any preternatural instantly, but only if I hit the brain or the heart. Given that this monster had kidnapped children to do God knows what with, I seriously doubted it had a heart.

Even above the retort of my pistols, I heard wood creaking. It took a few seconds for me to register that the crate had been lifted from the floor. The beast raised it like cardboard and tossed it like a tennis ball.

I kept firing and backpedaled as fast as I could before I dodged a flying box. A split second later, it impacted against the floor and splintered. Large slats of wood flew like missiles in every direction. I managed to grab a skid and use it to shield myself from the barrage of jagged boards.

In an instant, the creature snatched the skid from my hands and stared down at me. With uncanny speed, it punched me in the throat. The sheer shock of the blow threatened to knock me unconscious. I suppose it was through enhanced adrenaline and sheer force of will that I wasn't out cold.

It let out another deafening roar and reached for me. I barely had time to fire my pistols into its face. Unfortunately, it used the skid as a shield and evaded a kill shot.

Before I could react, I felt the impact of the skid and the monster as it rammed me against the floor. I was pinned with no options for escape. The odor of rotting flesh and brimstone assaulted my nostrils, and I gagged.

Even though my arms were immobile, I could still flex my wrists. I angled the pistol in my right hand and concentrated to morph it into a sword. A satisfying thud and an inhuman howl of pain told me I'd been successful in wounding it.

The creature raised up and staggered back. Apparently, I hadn't punctured its heart, but at least I'd gotten its attention. I used the moment to fire the pistol in my left hand.

It raised its gigantic arms to deflect the shots and in one leap reached the skylight and vanished. I took in some deep breaths and made sure it wasn't coming back.

I looked up and realized that the little girl still hung there. I suppose I'll take my victories where I can get them. I just had to figure out how to get her down.

A hero's work is never done.

———

As the little girl and I made our way to the mouth of the alley, I spotted at least half a dozen police officers, their weapons drawn and trained on us. In the center of them, a tall figure stood next to a shorter one. They were silhouetted against the spotlights and flashers from the three squad cars I could see.

"Drop any weapons and advance slowly with your hands where we can see them," Jazz' baritone rang out.

"It's Ivory Blaque. I've got the girl," I struggled to yell. My throat was still raw from my adversary's punch to the throat.

"Ivory?" Jazz slowly advanced, his weapons still drawn but lowered. "Hold your fire, men, that means you, too, Andy."

Detective Jazz Fitzgerald and Detective Andy Glowiak were partners in the Unexplained Crimes Unit of the Chicago Police Department. They investigated any crimes or sightings involving preternaturals.

As far as the general public was concerned; vampires, lycans, fae, ghosts and goblins, were the stuff of fairy tales and Hollywood horror. The officers of the UCU and I knew better.

"Is the victim alive?" Jazz was now within a couple of yards from me.

I swallowed to help my damaged voice. "Yes, but unconscious. We should get her looked at immediately."

Jazz took her from my arms and handed her to a uniformed officer who had advanced behind him. He flipped out a flashlight and looked at me.

"What about you, are you all right?"

"I'll be fine," I managed. "But we need to talk, privately."

He nodded and helped me out of the alley. "I understand."

————

At Jazz' insistence, I let the EMT's check me out. By the time they got around to me, most of my more serious injuries had already begun to heal. They advised I go to a hospital, which I vehemently declined.

We made it to the precinct in Bronzeville, which Jazz and Andy worked out of, around 11 PM. The office looked like a mini police bullpen, with seven large desks situated throughout the room. The unit consisted of Jazz as unit commander, Andy as his vice commander, four active field detectives and one house mouse—a desk jockey who worked their dispatch.

I ran down the details of my encounter with Santa's reindeer from hell. Jazz steadily pecked at his keyboard while Andy made plenty of "hmphs" and gave me occasional nods in between.

"So exactly what the hell was that thing, anyway," I asked.

After several more seconds of typing, Jazz swiveled the monitor of his terminal towards me with a drawing that closely resembled the creature I'd fought.

"Oh my God, that's it!"

Jazz nodded. "According to the database, this preternatural is known as a Krampus."

"I'm familiar with the legend of the Krampus. According to German folklore, a beast would kidnap all of the bad kids and take them to his lair to torture and eventually eat them." I said.

Jazz nodded. "It has been referred to as the "Anti-Claus" by some. We always knew that, of the nearly eight hundred thousand kids that go missing worldwide, about a third are due to rogue preternaturals. Based on the data I found in the archives, Krampuses have been particularly elusive. In fact, we have no photographs and no eyewitness accounts of these creatures...until tonight."

"In other words, I'm the only person to encounter this preternatural child abductor—who's successfully eluded humans over the past few centuries—and lived to tell about it. Lucky me."

Jazz gave me a wan grin and leaned back in his chair. He looked from me to Andy and back again. "So, since you've lived to tell the tale, would you mind helping us track it down and find the missing children?"

Andy sat silently while he sipped his coffee and read an issue of Sports Illustrated. Not that I'd have wanted to hear his two cents, anyway. He's been giving me the cold shoulder ever since [simple half sentence summary.]

"In for a penny, in for a pound. At least that's what my Papa used to say," I said.

Jazz grinned. "Good, now let's put together a plan to track down this monster."

———

An evening of Christmas shopping had turned into a job for the Chicagoland Preternatural Magistrate. Since getting Malik a gift before Christmas Day was now out of the question, I figured, what better way to spend time with my lycan boyfriend than to recruit him for my latest endeavor?

Because of his keen sense of smell and my close encounter with the Krampus, he isolated the creature's scent easily, as did six of his wolves. They scoured Lincoln Square and outlying areas for it and kept in contact with me and the detectives via radio.

Jazz had formed a small network of uniformed officers who worked with the UCU to patrol the neighborhood and monitor any reported incidents of missing children. Hopefully, between me, the detectives, the uniformed officers, Malik and his wolves, we could track down the Krampus.

"I think I've got something," Malik's voiced buzzed in my earpiece.

"Go ahead, Tokugawa," Jazz chimed.

"The creature's scent gets stronger the farther we get into Winnemac Park. It's my guess that this would be the most likely place for it to have a lair. It's centrally located, near the major streets and there are copses around the park to hide in."

"Clear, we'll move in cautiously," Jazz replied.

———

The traffic had died down and most shoppers had made their way home. I started to sprint—as best I could through the fallen snow—to Winnemac, when a green taxi with a silver crown painted on the rear door pulled up beside me.

"Hop in, Lass, I'll give ye a ride to yer destination," the cabbie said.

"How do you know where I'm headed?"

He grinned. "There ain't much in the way of travel I don't know, Milady. But time is of the essence if ye want to catch the beastie that's been snatching up the city's youth this eve."

How the hell did this old fart know about the Krampus or that I was after him?

For some reason, an inner voice told me I could trust him, so I got into the cab. He turned his profile to me and that's when I noticed the tin foil crown he wore. Either he'd volunteered at nearby children's hospital or he'd escaped from a looney bin. The way my night's been going, both scenarios are plausible.

"Allow me ta introduce meself. I'm called the Transit King," he said with an impish grin and an outstretched hand.

I pursed my lips and raised an eyebrow. "Transit King?"

"Aye. I watch over the 'ways, I help those in need, in return for favors owed. An' I try ta keep the 'supernatural' apart from ye humans as best I can."

I nodded and shook his hand. He continued to grip my hand in his as he spoke. "I see. Well, I know you're connected with the Fae, so I suppose I can buy some of your story."

The Transit King's eyes twinkled as he nodded. "Smart lass. I understand yer after a Krampus, and I'm here to offer me assistance."

I felt a tingle in my hand. He must have felt it too, because he brusquely released my hand, turned back around and moved the cab forward. He scrutinized me in the rearview mirror.

"Yer one special lady, I can tell."

I returned his scrutiny as he made his way to Lincoln Square. His aura burned a bit brighter than before in the dim light of the cab.

"Usually, people in need ask favors of me, an' then they owe me. I'm offerin' a favor for a favor."

I smirked. "I haven't asked you for jack. But, what makes you think I need a favor from you?"

He reached into his glovebox at the next stoplight and pulled out a bundle of dark red cloth. He handed it to me through the window in the plexiglass divider.

"What the hell is this?"

The Transit King smiled. "Open it up and see for yeself, Lass."

I carefully untied the cord and unfolded the cloth to reveal a large opulent looking ring made of silver with a stone that resembled a garnet centered in it. Even in the dull light from the streetlamps, it sparkled like a red diamond.

"Sorry, but I'm already engaged," I said.

The Transit King erupted in raucous laughter.

"Yer the second lass ta take what I offered in that manner. Nae, nothin' of th' sort, Lass! Marriage isn't fer the likes of me. Anyways, be sure not to place the ring on ye finger until ye are ready for battle."

I gave him a blank stare. "Okay, why is that?"

"Ye'll learn soon enough, Lass/."

"I see. You never did say what you expect to get in return. What exactly would I owe you?"

The Transit King's smile brightened. "When the time is nigh, I will call on ye. Until then, be on yer way to vanquish the foul beast."

I got out of the cab and turned back to look at the Transit King. "When this is over, how will I get this ring back to you?"

He winked at me with a sly grin. "I'll be staying with me friend over the holidays. His name be Connor O'Quinn, although ye may know him as Stone. Return it to me there; ye know the way."

Without another word, he sped off down the road and seemed to vanish at the end of the block. What a strange old man.

Four CPD patrol cars—no lights, no sirens—pulled up and parked horizontally in the intersections to the left and right of the main entrance off XXX Street.

I turned to enter the park and experienced a disturbance in

the force. The same hornet stings and queasiness I felt when I first encountered the Krampus.

Jazz' voice chimed in my ear. "Ivory, we've surrounded the park. Malik, have you determined the approximate location of its lair?"

"No, it seems to fluctuate rapidly. I'm beginning to think it may have gone underground. My wolves are moving in from every corner of the park towards the center," Malik replied.

I pursed my lips and scanned the area. "Are there any signs of the children?"

There was a long silence before Malik and Jazz answered in unison. "No."

Damn, a lump formed in my stomach as bile rose to my throat. "I'm going in."

The hairs on the nape of my neck stood on end and my skin was a sheet of gooseflesh. After my first encounter with the Krampus, I'd be lying if I said I was looking forward to another. I only hoped that this trinket the Transit King loaned me would work. Then again, I could be buying into the grand delusions of a crazy old man, even though level of Fae mojo he emitted somewhat validated his claims.

Ten yards into the park, the tiny pinpricks of preternatural energy bombarded me, like the nibbling of one hundred fire ants on my flesh.

It was almost enough to turn me back, but the images of that poor woman whose daughter I rescued popped into my head. The look of helplessness and sheer horror when the Krampus had her child would forever be burned into my mind. I thought of the other parents as equally worried about kids. I had to find those children and stop this creature.

The intensity increased the closer I got to the center of the park. A cluster of snow-covered trees with gnarled lifeless branches stood as harbingers to what I knew lay ahead. The snow crunched beneath my feet with every step I took.

I scanned the area, but saw no sign of the Krampus, not even tracks in the snow. The park was eerily silent. I strained to listen for any sound that might alert me to the monster's presence. Nothing.

In mid-step, a rush of air hit me before the huge distorted figure leapt from beneath the snow and hung in mid-air for what seemed like an eternity. Its gaped maw revealed large fangs that glistened even in the dim light from the sparse lamps throughout the park. The soiled Santa suit—even snow covered—resembled a flat gray version of the department store Santas.

A blood curdling roar sounded as it descended on me. I barely had time to roll away from where it landed in a plume of snow. I took advantage of the seconds and placed the ring on my finger. My vision wobbled, and for a brief second, time seemed to come to a complete standstill. A bizarre tingle shot through my body and I watched as my clothing morphed.

I found myself in a beyond-skimpy version of Santa's coat that barely covered my ass cheeks, a Santa hat and large black cavalier boots with a buckle on them. I went from festive holiday shopper's garb to Santa's Ho.

Seriously? What the hell?

The Krampus turned towards me and its eyes grew large, apparently as appalled at my garment as I was.

"I am Nicholas, Bishop of Myra and protector of children," a disembodied voice said.

For a split second, I thought I'd lost my mind, but as I stood there in this sexy Santa get up and faced a hellish monster Santa, I digressed.

The Krampus swiped a massive claw at me and sent me flying into a snow bank several yards away. I landed in a billowing cloud of snow. My visibility sucked, and when I looked up, the beast was gone.

"Rise mortal, we must vanquish this foul demon before the clock strikes midnight, or the souls of his captives will be forfeit!"

"That's easier said than done Saint Nick. What do you have in mind, anyway?"

"Use your weapons as blades, they are far more formidable in that configuration. I will bestow upon you my power so that you may slay this beast and send it back to hell."

I slowly stood and shook the snow from my body. I took the God Killers from their holsters and concentrated. They shimmered and elongated as they transformed from pistols to long swords. A shock of raw power coursed through my body. I felt at least twice as strong. Arcs of energy danced from the surface of my weapons.

In that moment, Malik and three of his wolves padded towards me in the snow, hackles raised, and fangs bared. They had assumed their four-legged forms and looked at me with eyes that glowed amber.

As they made their way to me, an eddy of snow swirled between us and, in a loud explosion, the Krampus reappeared. Malik and his wolves leapt at the monster and tore viciously at it. Savage growls escaped their throats and the Krampus responded in kind. I resisted the urge to jump into the fray, as I didn't want to strike my allies.

With a herculean shrug, the Krampus twisted its massive body and sent the wolves flying away. Sharp yelps rang out as they hit nearby trees with enough force to crack them.

"Malik!"

My heart leapt into my throat.

"Strike now, Mortal, while the demon is momentarily weakened," Nick said.

Unrestrained fury coiled within me as I charged the monster at full speed. I slashed at its gigantic limbs with a celerity I'd never experienced before. My eyes couldn't focus on my own movements, they were so fast.

Bits of fabric and demonic flesh flew from the Krampus. The odor of brimstone burned my nostrils as plumes of smoke rose from the beast's body. Each strike resulted in a flash of energy that was almost blinding. Deep from within my core, raw power surged to the surface and in one swift double-bladed arc, I severed its head and pierced its heart.

I took a step back and watched as the remains of the Krampus smoked and sizzled until it evaporated into the air. Smoldering ash and scorched earth were the only traces of the monster left.

My heart raced as I looked at my watch. It read twelve oh one.

God, I was too late.

A second later, I heard cries for help and coughing. It seemed to come from below the surface. I sheathed my swords and raced in the direction of the sounds. I furiously dug into the snow and scooped it away to reveal a hole in the ground.

The first cherubic fact I saw belonged to a little girl, no older than five. She reached out and grabbed me around my neck.

"Santa, I knew you'd come to save us!"

I wrapped my arms around her and squeezed her tight as dozens of other children crawled from the hole and gathered around me. Each of them shouted, danced and took turns hugging me. A tear ran down my cheek and a warm sensation spread through my body.

As the last of the two dozen children emerged from the ground, I looked to where the wolves had fallen. They were gone. Pangs of guilt rushed over me for not having checked on them sooner. Although the thought that they had survived their encounter with the Krampus made the moment that much sweeter.

"You have done well, Mortal."

I smirked. "Yeah, you didn't do too bad yourself, Old Saint Nick."

———

Two hours later, after I had released the children to Jazz and explained my change in attire, I made my way back to my condo in Hyde Park.

I called Malik and told him to meet me at my place in an hour. When I got home and looked in the full-length mirror in my bedroom, despite my battle with the Krampus, my outfit was surprisingly as clean as whistle. I did, however, take a shower, put on a Bing cherry shade lipstick, sprayed on some

Bond No 9 Signature perfume and slid my feet into a pair of black leather, strappy heels.

I put on some Will Downing and Anita Baker, lit some logs in the fireplace along with strategically placed candles. I opened a bottle of red wine, stretched out on top of my bed and waited.

Almost exactly an hour after I called him, Malik opened the bedroom door to me laying across my bed in my Sexy Santa garb with a large red ribbon wrapped around me and tied in a bow.

"Merry Christmas," I said, before taking a sip of wine.

Malik's eyes glowed amber and his aura blazed in the darkness of the bedroom. A rush of heat washed over me as my desire for him climbed.

He flashed a sly, lascivious grin. "Merry Christmas yourself, sexy."

I licked my lips and sat up on my side. He immediately took off his jacket and tossed it to the floor.

"I'm sorry I couldn't get you a proper gift."

My eyes lingered at his burgeoning crotch as I shuddered with lustful anticipation. He pulled off his clothing and stood at the foot of my bed in boxers with gingerbread men on them, staring at me. His sexy body looked as though it were made of pure caramel. Every muscle rippled and bulged on his Adonis-like form.

"Well, don't just stand there. Come unwrap your gift."

He climbed onto the bed and pulled at the bow to unwrap me.

"Taa-daa! Ivory Santa at your service," I said, as he jumped on top of me.

We kissed. Our tongues danced while we caressed each other as his lycan power roiled against my skin. "I thought you said you didn't have time to get me a present?"

I grinned. "You're looking at it Pal. I would suggest that you start unwrapping it now."

His eyes narrowed with a sexy grin on his lips. "That's my favorite part." He began to remove my Santa suit, while his supple lips kissed my arched neck. We made love until sunrise and I had one of the best Christmases ever.

Thanks Saint Nick!

THE LEGEND OF MATCHEMONDEO

Twin Lakes, Indiana
Marshall Country; I-90
April 2015; 7:00pm

Rob Cloudfeather closed his eyes, but not because he was sleepy, although he had every cause to be after driving three hours straight on four hours of sleep. He closed his eyes because he wanted to concentrate. He wanted to find his quiet place, so that he could dig deep and muster up the strength to survive the weekend.

He'd even turned down his Mumford & Sons CD as he waited for Chris to come out of the Qwik-E Mart with the beer. That idiot had once again found a way to delay their arrival to the cabin. David, Josh and Rich were probably already there wondering what had kept them.

He didn't anticipate a fun weekend at Twin Lakes in the private cabin Josh's family owned. Rob would rather be at home in bed with a six pack of Guinness and a fat joint, than hanging out with a group of people in the middle of nowhere. Like that scenario usually works out well.

He found himself in this predicament all because of a stupid bet. If only he had left well enough alone, but no, he let it all ride on the last hand of poker. Now, not only had he lost a good portion of his rent money to Chris, but the only recourse at his disposal to win the money back—according to Josh—had been to spend the weekend in the woods with a group of rich assholes who only hung out with him because his parents had won the lottery twelve years ago.

He'd thought about simply asking his parents for the money, but he didn't want to hear another lecture from his father on how he needed to grow up, make more mature decisions and take responsibility for his actions. Like his Dad had become the paragon of responsibility and maturity. The only reason he'd won the lottery in the first place was because he'd gotten fired from his job of thirty years for coming in to work drunk. In his stupor, he spent his last money on a Powerball ticket and hit the jackpot of $10,000,000.

Rob's mother put the money to good use and invested a good portion of it, which resulted in their now being worth one hundred times what they'd started with. She threatened to leave his Dad and take every last penny if he didn't sober up and be more responsible. Now that he'd been clean for just over a decade, suddenly he could preach to Rob about making good decisions, yeah right.

He opened his eyes and looked into the store for Chris,

when he saw a large Native American man standing next to the entrance. He stared at Rob with his arms folded across his massive chest. The man wore a large black brimmed hat, a black duster, blue jeans and black cowboy boots.

Rob looked back at him and wondered why he stared at him. He looked away and tried to play it off by turning up the volume on his stereo, but when he looked back the man still stared at him. Their eye contact lingered until the man walked towards the vehicle. He rolled down his window a crack.

"Nekane," the man said, as he walked past the vehicle.

"What did you say?" Rob asked.

He craned his neck to look in the direction that the man had headed.

"Okay, let's roll," Chris said, as he opened the door and hopped into Rob's Hummer with two cases of beer.

"Jesus dude, what the hell?" Rob said.

"What the fuck is it now?"

"You just scared the shit outta me."

"Sorry man. What's got you so jumpy?"

Rob looked back in the direction the man walked off in and he had vanished.

"There was some big creepy Native dude standing around out there. Didn't you see him when you came out of the store?"

"Native? You mean a hick?"

"No, Native American. You know like an Indian," Rob said.

"All of these stores are owned by Indians. The guy behind the counter sounded like that character on the Simpsons. He even asked me if I wanted a purple slushy," Chris said.

Rob glared at Chris, who had the same damned clueless look on his face as he always had. He'd probably forgotten that Rob was half Native American.

"What?" Chris said.

Rob decided to not waste his breath on trying to explain. "Never mind, let's just go," he said, as he turned up the volume.

As they pulled out onto I-90, Chris immediately ejected Rob's CD and tossed it in the back seat.

"What the fuck man?"

"Dude, you're not seriously expecting me to ride for another hour listening to that Hillbilly bullshit, are you?" Chris said.

Rob's hands tightened on the steering wheel as he fought the urge to reach over and bitch slap this asshole.

"Haven't I taught you anything about music in the past twelve years I've known you? You have to roll to road trip music," Chris said, as he took out a CD from his case, popped it in the car player and turned up the volume.

The loud electric guitar of AC/DC's "Highway to Hell" blasted through the stereo speakers. Rob liked the band, but he wasn't really in the mood.

He hit the door control and slid down the driver's side window. He glanced over at Chris, engaged in an air guitar solo which resembled a fish out of water, flailing about in its fight to breathe.

Rob hit the eject button on the CD player, took the disc and tossed it out of the window.

"What the fuck Dude," Chris whined.

"Haven't I taught you anything in the twelve years I've

known you? Never touch my goddamn CD player," Rob said, as he slid his window back up.

Chris looked at Rob with his eyes wide and his mouth opened. He reached into his backpack and pulled out his mp3 player.

"Fine, be a dick. You still have to win back your money or listen to your old man bitch about how much of a screw up you are."

"Yeah, but at least I'll listen to my own damned music in my own damned car," Rob said.

Chris flipped him the bird, put his ear buds in, turned around in his seat and poked out his lip.

In all honesty, the silence was golden for Rob. Chris tended to run on about some of the silliest shit for hours at a time. He simply wasn't in the mood for any of it. His recent break up with Peg had been rough. They'd been together since high school, but where she wanted to get married with the white picket fence and the house on the hill, Rob just wanted to be chill.

He wanted to experience life and explore the various possibilities out in the world. He loved her, but he wasn't feeling the idea of being tied down so young. Besides, his parents thought she had only been after his money.

Fat lot of good the money would be to him or her for that matter, seeing as it was tied in a trust until he turned twenty-five, more than two years from now.

After an hour, Chris had fallen asleep and Rob could be at peace with his thoughts. He reached into his jacket pocket for his pack of cigarettes. Rob placed one between his pinched lips, reached for his lighter and lit it. He slid down the window a ways and took it from his mouth to blow the smoke out.

The nicotine helped to relax him even more as they made their way south. He needed the cool spring evening air to help keep him awake as well as let in some fresh air. It would be the only one he'd get to have for a while because of Rich's allergy to smoke.

Pussy, Rob thought.

He hadn't passed another vehicle in almost five miles. Even with the brights on, he could barely see fifteen feet in front of him for the shadows of the trees. The woods were dark on both sides of the road as the setting sun had completed its descent below the horizon.

Rob caught a glimpse of movement in his headlights. Glowing eyes stared back at him as a creature skittered across the road.

Oh my God there's an ugly monster out there, Rob thought.

He swerved to avoid running over it and caused the Hummer to jostle them as they came to a stop on the side of the road.

"What the fuck," Chris said.

"There was something in the road."

Chris looked around for anything out of the usual. He saw two glowing eyes followed by a long, narrow tail slink off into the woods.

"Man, it's just an opossum. Quit being such a girl." Chris said.

"Shut up and take your dumb ass back to sleep," Rob said, as he attempted to swallow his heart which was lodged in his throat.

"Wuss," Chris said, as he snuggled back into a comfortable position.

"Prick," Rob said, as he continued down the dark road.

————

They got to the cabin at 8pm. The early spring sky was black except for the full moon which decided to peak out from behind the clouds now and then.

The huge cabin stood two stories, had a wraparound porch and two large, shuttered, outcropping bay windows upstairs. Dim lights shined through the windows giving the front of the cabin the appearance of a sinister face.

First the opossum, now the creepy looking cabin in the woods, Rob wondered what would be next.

Rob pulled up beside Josh's black Denali and turned off the engine. There were lights and loud music coming from the cabin, which let Rob know that their gathering was in full effect.

"Wake up, dip shit, we're here."

Chris snorted before he started awake. He looked around in a daze and sat there with an odd look on his face.

"Are you coming or what?" Rob said.

"I gotta piss, Dude."

Rob looked at him and shook his head.

"So go piss then, who's stopping you?"

"I'm scared."

"Man, are you serious? I'm sure there's a toilet in the cabin just wait until we're inside."

"I gotta go now," Chris said.

"So what do you want me to do, hold it?"

Chris stared at Rob with the same blank look he had at the Qwik-E Mart. "Would you?"

Rob looked at him, shook his head, reached into the glove box, pulled out a flashlight and threw it into his lap.

"There you go, your new best friend."

"Fine, but if anything happens to me, I'm holding you responsible," Chris said.

"Bite me," Rob said, as he grabbed his duffel bag and a case of beer. "Oh, and be sure to get your shit out of my car and bring the rest of the beer in."

Chris trotted off towards the woods with his middle finger prominently displayed. Rob smirked, shook his head and made his way to the cabin.

Rob heard the thumping bass of some rap music coming from the other side of the door. He sat down the beer on the porch and was about to knock on the door when it opened.

"Hey there, cutie," a tall blonde said.

Rob wanted to look her in the eyes, but her bountiful breasts had mesmerized him.

"Hi," Rob said.

"You must be Rob, Josh told us you were coming," she said. "My name is Tricia."

She held out her hand and smiled. Rob looked up into her large blue eyes and stared at her. Her teeth were perfect and sparkling white. She looked like a swimsuit model he'd seen in a Sports Illustrated magazine once.

Tricia wore a pink, tight fitting t-shirt, gray sweatpants and sneakers. Her long hair flowed down her shoulders in a wave.

"Are you going to shake my hand and come inside?" Tricia asked.

"Huh? Oh, I'm sorry," Rob shook her hand, and then picked up the case of beer before he stepped inside.

The main room of the cabin looked like a ski lodge. A fire burned in the fireplace which gave the room a warm and cozy atmosphere.

"Well, look who finally showed up," Josh bellowed from across the room. His sun bleached, blonde hair contrasted with his tanned complexion. He had the lithe, yet muscled physique of a surfer and the trophies to boot.

Josh walked towards Rob and clasped him in a bear hug.

"I think she likes you," he whispered into Rob's ear.

"Hey girls, meet my best buddy Rob," Josh said.

Rob inwardly cringed at his host's pretentiousness. They were anything but best buddies. In fact, Rob didn't even particularly like Josh Dupree or his family. Dupree Developments had recently bought up the land in this area in order to build a Native American Casino and Theme Park, complete with a three-story shopping mall and actors in red face, dressed in buckskin. The shameless exploitation of his ancestors alone was cause for disliking Josh, but his being a Grade "A" asshole only exacerbated his abhorrence.

"Hi Rob," the girls said in unison.

Rob turned to see David and Rich seated next to a dark skinned brunette and a redhead.

The dark-skinned girl introduced herself as Sasha and the redhead as Terri. On the other sofa next to them sat a slightly plump Goth chick named Lori and another gorgeous blonde named Courtney, who introduced themselves.

"We thought you'd chickened out," David said, with a smirk.

"Yeah, we thought you and your boyfriend decided to stay home and spoon," Rich said. His curly mop of blonde hair, chubby face and ruddy complexion made him look like a fat cherub.

Rich gave David a fist bump and they cackled like two crows.

"Very funny. I see you and your husband are still together, although I'm not certain why you're letting these ladies get between your bromance."

The girls giggled as both David and Rich flipped off Rob.

"Where's Chris?" Josh asked.

"That fucker said he had to take a piss. He should be coming in soon with the rest of the beer," Rob said.

There were three sofas which formed a U in front of the fireplace. Rob and Tricia sat on the one across from where David, Rich and the girls sat.

"Usually, it's just us guys who get together up here and play poker all weekend, but I thought we'd do things differently this time. So, I invited you girls to join us," said Josh.

There goes my opportunity to win back the money I lost, Rob thought.

"Tonight, I'm going to tell you all a scary story," Josh said, then paused.

The entire room busted out in laughter.

"Are you gonna tuck us in too, when it's time to go to bed?" Rich said.

"No, but if I did it would be the only tucking you'd see all weekend."

"Ohhh," David said.

"But first, let's get this party started right," Josh said, as he pulled out a large joint from his shirt pocket.

"Dammit Josh, you know I'm allergic to smoke," Rich said.

Josh mocked him in a whiny voice and shook the joint in front of his face.

"That's it, I'm going outside," Rich said.

"Go outside, pussy," Josh said.

Rich grabbed Terri's hand and they headed outside.

Josh sat down and lit it, then took a long drag. He held it in for seven seconds before he exhaled. The acrid smoke billowed from his nostrils and spread across the room.

"Dude, not cool," Rob said.

"Do you want to join him, or are you gonna be a man and have some fun."

"Fine, but aren't we gonna at least wait for Chris?" Rob said.

"Fuck him. He's probably passed out in your ride, drunk out of his mind," Josh said,

"He better not be."

Rob started to get up and go outside, but Josh reached out with his arm.

"Dude, just relax. Everything's gonna be just fine."

———

Chris drank the last of his beer. He was six cans deep out of twenty-four. He didn't have long before Josh led everyone outside.

The tool shed had been located exactly where Josh said it would be. And the refrigerator had been fully stocked with beer. A large bear skin hung up on the wall. He reached out and grabbed it. The odor of diesel fuel, mold and stirred dust made him cough.

He took the bear skin and flipped it around his shoulders. He looked at his reflection in the mirror of the tractor and laughed.

"Booga, booga, booga," he said, as he danced around the tool shed.

He grabbed another beer from the fridge and guzzled it. He made his way to the door and peeped out. The light from the cabin could barely be seen in the distance.

"This is gonna be good," Chris snickered.

He stopped in his tracks. A scratching noise came from behind the tool shed outside. Chris listened for it again.

It was probably a raccoon or something, he thought.

As he made his way out of the shed, he heard the noise again. He hoped that he hadn't messed things up by coming out too late. He made his way past a pile of firewood and around the back of the shed. He saw nothing but a large tree whose branches stretched out to the shed. The wind rustled the leaves and the branches swayed.

It must have been the sound of the branches scraping the outside of the shed, he thought.

He turned to sneak down to the cabin and stopped short when he saw a man standing a few feet away. The scarce moonlight which filtered between the tree limbs, doused the figure in a silvery aura.

Chris was shocked. He hadn't expected to see anyone out here so soon.

"Hey Josh, am I too late," he said.

The figure stood silently watching him. Its eyes glowed bright red and it made a low, eerie high-pitched sound. Chris rubbed his eyes and shook his head. He must have been drunker than he'd thought.

"Hey, this isn't funny Josh. I'm sorry if I screwed things up," he said.

The figure walked towards him with an odd gait, as though it weren't entirely comfortable walking upright. As it grew closer, Chris saw what he had thought to be fur covering its body. He noticed an odd odor like when matches were lit, only tinged with rotting meat.

A tendril of ice-cold fear snaked along his spine. He wanted to scream and move, but found himself rooted in place. His mouth hung open; only the lump in his throat prevented him from making a sound.

What in the hell is this thing? he wondered. *Was it a bear? But there hadn't been any bears in Indiana for over one hundred years, he thought.*

Chris remembered the flashlight Rob had given him, reached into his pocket with nervous hands and fumbled to find the switch. The figure stopped three feet in front of him before he finally flicked on the light.

He moved the path of the light towards the figure and was greeted with a loud grunt. He saw its face in the beam. Shaggy hair hung down from its head, snarling fangs slickened with saliva bared at him. Its maw wasn't as elongated as a bear, more like an ape. It reared away from the light in the split second before it swiped at Chris and sent him flying into the back of the shed.

Chris felt the grooves etched into his cheek and tasted the warm metallic flavor of blood as it welled in his mouth. He gasped for a breath, but none would come. He felt his legs twitch uncontrollably and a cold chill ran through his body.

He managed to look up as the creature loomed closer. Its red eyes burned into his mind as it reached out and grabbed him by the throat. He felt his body jerk violently before he faded to black.

————

The creature shook him again, as though puzzled by his stillness. It grunted, then raised its head to the sky and made its eerie cry again.

The sound of a door slamming and voices in the distance caught its attention. The beast peered around the corner of the shed and saw movement from the cabin. It tossed Chris' dead body onto the pile of firewood and watched intently as two figures ran into the woods.

————

By the time Josh started the story; the joint had made three rounds and had come back for a fourth. Everyone had had at least two beers and whiskey shots were making the rounds as well.

Josh stood on shaky legs and held up his hands.

"Okay everybody, it's story time."

The din of laughter and music filled the air and his call for silence fell on deaf ears. He nudged Courtney and motioned for her to turn down the music.

She stared at him with a blank expression, then finally stumbled over to the stereo and turned down the volume.

"Okay folks, it's story time."

Slowly the voices in the room died down and everyone focused their attention on Josh. Rob was the only one of them not plastered and that had only been because he'd snacked while he drank his beer.

"Okay, so like here's the story. Years ago, like back in the 1800's, the government wanted to relocate Indians from their homes, out to like Kansas somewhere. They called it the Trail of Sorrow, and it started up north and made its way down through Indiana."

"It's called the Trail of Death," Rob corrected him.

"Thanks, Top Nerd!"

Rob held up his bottle of beer and flipped him off.

Tricia grabbed his arm and smiled at him, he smiled back.

Rob hated when people didn't know their history, especially when it came to Native Americans. His father was a Potawatomi and had ancestors who survived the relocation. Some of them moved back to Indiana and now live up north in LaPorte County.

"Anyway, some of the Indians who traveled along the trail became ill and died. There had been a priest who went with them named Benjamin Petit. He prayed for the sick and saw to the burials of those who died. He became friends with a shaman who traveled with them along the trail. When many of the travelers in his group died, the shaman took those remaining, deserted the trail and migrated southeast. They eventually took up residence in these very woods. A small group of army soldiers followed their trail in an effort to bring them in. Not many of the deserters survived and were buried somewhere in the woods. It is believed that the shaman called upon the Great Spirit Kitchemonedo to protect them, however, he cursed the land by calling upon the Evil Spirit Matchemonedo to drive away anyone who dared to set foot here."

———

Rich and Terri could barely contain their laughter as they trotted away from the cabin. They held hands and playfully button hooked around trees. They were to play a big role in the festivities Josh had in store for the evening. At first, Terri had been reluctant until she found out that the plan would have the two of them alone in the woods for at least a half hour. Long enough to get laid and play their part in Josh's plan.

"Do you think they bought it," Terri said.

"Of course they did. Even as much of a fuck up as Chris is, he'd have a hard time messing up Josh's plan. This is gonna be so much fun."

Terri smiled at Rich. They'd only been dating for a few months, but she found something about him irresistible. Every time they were alone, she had to have him, no matter the place or time.

She reached out and started to kiss him. At first it was slow and exploratory, and then it got heated. Rich caressed her ass while she worked at unfastening his pants.

Once she had his pants unfastened and pulled down, she

pushed him away. They maintained eye contact as she slid her sweatpants down, followed by her panties, turned towards a tree and balanced herself against it.

She waited for him to enter her and he did. She had been more than wet enough from the time they left the cabin. His engorged manhood filled her every crevice. They found their rhythm and maintained it with each stroke.

Between the sound of his hips against her ass and her own moans, she almost didn't hear the sound of snapping twigs and rustled leaves, like someone approaching. She tried to look around but saw no one. At that point she really didn't care.

"Did you hear something," Terri moaned.

"Yeah, I heard you cumming."

Terri heard a loud grunt and an odd howl. Rich stopped and she saw a blur of movement to her right. She watched as something round hit the ground and bounced around.

She turned around and saw Rich fall away from her, to be replaced with a dark silhouette. Terri scrambled to pull up her pants and saw a hair covered beast.

She screamed and tried to run, but the monster grabbed her, and she fell to the ground. What she'd seen earlier had landed upright and she realized it was Rich's head.

Massive hands gripped Terri, pulled her off the ground and turned her over.

Frozen with fear, she stared in the creature's savage visage. Ropes of saliva hung on its fangs and glistened in the silvery moonlight when it roared. Its eyes glowed amber and flashed with unspeakable rage.

Terri screamed at the top of her lungs for the split second before a sharp pain bit her. Her body twitched uncontrollably, shrouded with the deepest of chills. As she lay there gurgling on her blood, she watched the monster as it feasted on the flesh of her throat and she slipped into death.

———

Josh stood by the fireplace and glanced at his watch.

What is that idiot doing? He should have been here by now. Knowing that jackass, he'd probably gotten drunk and passed out in the shed, he thought.

Soft arms wrapped around his waist and a warm body clung to his back. The gentle scent of honeysuckle met his nostrils and he knew it was Courtney.

She had proven to be the best lay he had ever had. Her father owned one of the largest logistics companies in Indiana and she was a star cheerleader in Bloomington. She was also prettier than any other girl he'd ever seen.

"What's on your mind?"

"Nothing, I'm okay," Josh said.

"Bullshit. We've been dating for over a year and I know when something's got you twisted. Fess up now or no goodies for you later."

Josh hated when women used sex to get their way. Although given how good it was with Courtney, he always found himself giving in.

"I had something cool planned and it fell through. I…"

A loud crash from outside reverberated throughout the cabin. Everyone stopped and turned towards the front door.

Josh went to the stereo and turned down the music.

"What the hell was that?" David exclaimed.

Silence lingered.

Josh shrugged. "I don't know, why don't you go check it out?"

"Me, why me? It's your cabin."

"Don't be a pussy, David, and go check it out!"

David stood and looked around the room as all eyes were riveted on him. He walked cautiously towards the door and turned to glare at Josh.

"Sure, send the black guy out to investigate. We all know how this usually goes," David said.

"Honey be careful," Sasha said.

"Here take this," Josh said, as he handed David a fireplace poker.

David snatched it from Josh's hand and slowly opened the front door.

The chilled air crept in from the doorway, the breeze whipped up some leaves, which made their way into the cabin. David darted his head left to right as he took slow, tentative steps out onto the porch. His hand tightened on the poker as he held it out like a club.

"I don't see anything, guys," David said.

A nervous smirk spread across Josh's face. "I'm sure it's just Chris, Rich and Terri fucking with us."

Rob shook his head and took a swig of beer. Chris was an immature turd, everyone knew that. But he'd bet his last dollar that Josh was in on whatever was going on.

David turned back towards the doorway and in a blink of an eye, he was snatched off the porch. The poker clanged to the floor as his screams mingled with a savage roar.

The frightened group gathered at the entrance as Sasha ran to the porch. "David," she yelled.

There was no reply as they stared into the darkness of the woods.

"Oh my God, David! We have to go after him," Sasha screamed.

Josh shook his head. "Fuck that! Look sister, he's your man. If you're so worried about him, why don't you go look for him?"

"Josh," Courtney exclaimed.

"Yeah man, don't be such a dick," Rob said.

Josh harrumphed. "What the fuck ever! I don't see any of you volunteering to go after him."

"Hey, where did Sasha go?" Lori asked.

They all turned their attention back outside. The wind howled in the darkness and rustled the leaves of the trees in the surrounding woods.

Rob noticed the nervous tension in Josh. He wondered if things had gotten out of hand in his silly prank to scare them. Tricia sidled up to him and slipped her hand into his.

"Rob, I'm scared," she said.

He squeezed her hand and looked over at her. "It's going to be alright. I think this is all Josh's doing, am I right?"

All eyes turned to Josh, who dipped his gaze to the floor.

"It was just supposed to be a prank. Chris was going to sneak around outside the cabin to frighten the girls, while I told scary tales here in the cabin. But he's been gone longer than we had planned and now, the others haven't come back either. I thought that maybe Chris had grabbed David, but now I'm not so sure."

"Oh no! Guys, this looks like blood," Lori said from the foot of the stairs.

A shadow rose from behind Lori and snatched her into the darkness.

"Help me," Lori shrieked.

The assembled group gasped as their friend screamed for her life. Savage growls and the sounds of erratic movement blended with Lori's cries. It ended in an abrupt silence, almost as quickly as it had begun.

"Everybody back inside," Rob yelled.

Courtney, Tricia and Josh heeded his command as he shut the door behind them and bolted it. He grabbed the two by four next to the door and securely wedged it into the brackets.

Courtney and Tricia huddled together on the sofa and cried, while Josh paced the floor in front of the fireplace. Rob stifled a thrill of terror as took a deep breath and tried to assess the situation as best he could.

"Whatever that thing out there is, it hasn't tried to make its way in here yet," Rob said.

Josh stopped and faced Rob. "So fucking what! It's only a matter of time before it does and when that happens its *game over,* man!"

Rob pointed a finger in Josh's direction and glared at him. "Pull it together, Josh! We have to arm ourselves against it. Does your family keep any hunting equipment in the cabin?"

Josh turned and opened a closet beneath the staircase. Inside, Rob made out a large metal gun safe. "My Dad and uncles keep a bow, a few rifles and a shotgun in here."

Josh worked the combination on the safe and opened it. He reached in and handed Rob the shotgun and one of the rifles. The other he kept for himself. He also grabbed boxes of ammunition and set them outside of the closet.

"I can use a bow," Tricia said, as she made her way from the sofa to where Rob and Josh stood.

Despite all that had happened, she seemed to be holding herself together pretty well, Rob noticed.

"I'm not sitting around here anymore. The cars are right outside, I say we make a run for it," Josh said.

Rob, Tricia and Courtney stood and made their way to the door behind Josh. They held their weapons at the ready and paused before Josh slowly opened the door.

The silence was deafening. The wind had come to a complete standstill and no animals could be heard. Inky darkness stretched beyond the rectangle of light cast on the porch from within the cabin.

"Do you guys hear that?" Rob said.

The others peered into the shadows and listened.

"I don't hear shit," Josh said.

Rob recognized the faint sounds of Native instruments far off in the distance. They were the same as those played by his many aunts and uncles during his summer visits to the casino and reservation in Marceau Bay as a kid.

Rob watched as the others listened to hear the sounds.

"I do hear sounds," Courtney said.

Tricia pointed off towards the distance, "Look, what's that?"

Rob peered in the direction she alerted them to and saw glowing, ethereal figures moving towards them. He strained to see that the spirits were dressed in the customary garb of his ancestors.

In a matter of seconds, the spirits advanced within fifty yards of the group. There was an assortment of men, women, and children amongst them. Despite his initial fear, sorrow welled up in Rob's heart at the sight of his people as they likely appeared on their trek during the Potawatomi Trail of Death.

"Screw this, let's get out of here," Josh said, as he grabbed Courtney's hand and headed to his car.

Josh fired his rifle at the apparitions with a crazed look in his eyes.

"No," Rob shouted.

The wind began to wail and mingled with the sounds of the ghosts. A loud guttural roar pierced the din and a shadow coalesced in front of Josh and Courtney. Moving clouds revealed the moon and in its light, the brutish figure could be seen clearly.

The beast stood at least seven feet tall and was about five feet wide. It resembled a cross between an ape and a bear, with a gaping maw of jagged ivory fangs and glowing red eyes. Thick, dark fur covered its massive body.

"What the fuck?" Josh said, as he opened fire on the monster.

Rob and Tricia watched in horror as the creature reached out its human-like hands with inhuman speed and ripped the weapon from Josh's grip. It snapped the rifle in two with its bare hands and roared at Josh, as spittle flew from its maw and covered him.

Courtney fumbled with her weapon as the beast grabbed

Josh's head with one hand and with a twist and pull, removed it from his shoulders. Rob watched as blood spurted from Josh's neck and his body fell to the ground in a heap.

Courtney screamed and dropped her weapon before she turned and ran back towards Rob and Tricia, who had already notched an arrow in her bow and fired an arrow at the creature. With incredible accuracy, the missive lodged in the monster's left eye. It bellowed in pain and reached up to remove the arrow.

Rob cocked his shotgun and fired at the creature, but it appeared to have little effect. Courtney stumbled and fell half way between Rob and the beast. It reached out, grabbed her leg and pulled her back towards it.

Courtney let out a frantic scream as she scrambled to get away. The monster hefted her into the air with its massive hands and pulled her apart at the waist. It tossed the two halves of what had been Courtney to the ground and released a thunderous roar.

Rob and Tricia stared in terror as he grabbed her hand and they ran as far as they could in the opposite direction. Both of them refused to look back at the horrific carnage they had just abandoned. Rob's mind raced at the thought of all that had happened. As tragic as the deaths of his friends had been, his primary concern at that moment was keeping he and Tricia alive.

Rob spotted an old shed in the clearing ahead of them.

"Let's hide in there," he said.

They reached the small shack and slipped inside. The interior was almost completely black, save for the faint glimmer of moonlight through a dirty, narrow window.

"We should be okay in here for a while," Rob said, as he reached into his pocket for his lighter.

He flicked it a couple of times before it caught. The interior of the shed was filled with various tools and landscaping equipment. The odor of gasoline mingled with motor oil, burned his nose.

"See if you can find a gas can," he said.

Tricia began to look around the shack and stumbled over something on the floor. The sound of cans rolling led Rob to shine the lighter's flame towards the ground where she stood.

"Beer cans," Tricia said.

Rob pursed his lips. He noticed they were recently drained and the same brand they'd gotten from the Qwik-E Mart. "Yeah, which means Chris was out here at some point tonight."

"That little shit," Tricia said.

Rob and Tricia hid at the opposite corners near the shed's entrance and waited. As the roaring of the beast died and was replaced by the howls of the wind, time seemed to stand still.

In a loud crash, the door of the shed flew open and revealed the dark silhouette of the beast in the doorway. It snarled and peered into the room. The stifling odor of brimstone merged with the gasoline and motor oil and threatened to make Rob retch.

It stepped inside and sniffed the air, as it scanned the room. Once it had made its way to the center of the shed, Tricia shouted, "Now," as she doused the creature with gasoline.

Rob slammed the butt of the rifle into the monster's face

several times and forced it back towards the rear of the shack. They ran out of the shack as Rob flicked his lighter and tossed it into the shed.

In a whoosh, fire spread through the interior of the tool shanty. Rob picked up a 2x4 and wedged it into the brackets outside of the door. In seconds, the entire structure was engulfed in flames.

Rob and Tricia watched as the shed burned and the beast inside roared with an agonizing din. Movement within the flames caught Rob's eye as a fiery figure burst from the burning shack and flailed in a frantic frenzy.

"Run," Rob said, as they again made their way through the woods. "If I remember correctly, the lake should be about another hundred yards in this direction."

They made their way to the lake, where a speed boat owned by Josh's family was docked. Rob helped Tricia into the craft as a loud bellow sounded, followed by the crashing of trees at the edge of the woods.

The moonlight revealed the smoldering beast, which stood and glared at them. The pungent odors of brimstone, burnt hair and flesh permeated the air and reached them over the distance. The ethereal figures gathered behind it and began to chant and play the spectral instruments.

"Hurry, they're coming for us," Tricia said.

Rob quickly untied the docking rope, hopped into the boat and pulled the cord on the motor. The creature was a several dozen yards away and closing fast.

After a few failed attempts to start the boat, the beast and his followers made their way to within less than twenty yards away.

"Hurry up," Tricia cried.

Rob ignored her and pulled the cord again. His efforts were met with the roar of the motor. They raced away from the shoreline as the monster and the apparitions closed the gap. Rob worried it would follow them into the water, but they remained frozen on the dock and stared after them as they sped across the lake.

An hour later, the sun had begun to rise and they made it to the other side of the lake, closest to I-90. Rob scanned the shore and there was no sign of anyone. He sprang from the boat, grabbed Tricia's hand and they sprinted towards the interstate and never looked back.

———

The rose madder sky along the eastern horizon peeked through the grayed lavender clouds, as the sun chased away the darkness.

Exhausted, Rob and Tricia fell into a heap at the edge of the road. He wrapped his left arm around her, as she laid her head on his chest. Rob felt her trembling, as her heart pounded in cadence with his own. Their shared experience had forged an unspoken bond between them.

A Marshall County Sherriff's Department car pulled up near them, its red and blue lights flashed, and their radiance pierced the shadows.

A deputy of average height exited the car and approached them on foot. "Morning, folks, what seems to be the problem?"

Rob looked up at the officer and used his right hand to shield his eyes. "We were attacked by a mon—"

Tricia nudged him in the ribs with her elbow before she spoke. "A homicidal maniac attacked us and our friends at the Dupree Cabin across the lake. We managed to escape, but our friends were hurt pretty bad."

The deputy gave them a cursory look before he keyed up his shoulder mike. "Dispatch, Adam-9 out on the western stretch of I-90 with one male, one female. Requesting an ambulance and back up. The couple reported a disturbance at the Dupree Cabin, could you send out a unit to check it out?"

"10-4," the dispatch operator said.

"You folks sit tight," the deputy said.

————

An hour later, Rob and Tricia sat in the back of an ambulance, huddled within blankets as EMT's attended to them. Several Marshall Country deputy cars had blocked off the eastbound lane of I-90. A few deputies stood several yards outside the perimeter, cordoned off with police tape.

A black SUV pulled up to the perimeter and a tall woman got out of the driver's side. She wore a charcoal gray pantsuit and a long, black leather car coat with leather gloves and black pumps.

Her bright red hair was medium length and framed her face beneath the black fedora atop her head. A determined set of her jaw was made even more ominous by the opaque shades which hid her eyes in the early dawn. She stopped to speak to one of the deputies and flashed him her badge and ID before she ducked under the yellow tape and strode towards them.

"Are you Robert Cloudfeather and Patricia Davidson?" she asked.

Rob and Tricia looked up at the woman and at each other before they spoke. "Yes," they said in nervous unison.

The woman held up her badge and ID. "My name is Rebecca Burton and I'm with the Special Investigations Unit, we need to talk."

THE ADVENTURES OF STAR BLAZER

August, 1959
Los Angeles, California

"Caution, Brick Sullivan, caution!" the Automaton blared.

A tall, dashing figure emerged from swirling clouds of smoke. He surveyed the room and spotted a prone woman on the floor a few feet ahead. He removed a shiny, full face helmet with a backward facing fin to reveal piercing, hazel eyes, dirty blond hair and a pencil thin moustache. He wore a brown leather tunic with a gold star emblem which consisted of a large gem emblazoned in its center, light gray trousers and black riding boots.

"Never fear A.T.O.M., I'm no stranger to danger," the man replied with a cheeky smile.

He stepped forward, leaned down and pulled the listless woman into his arms. Her eyes fluttered before they opened wide in a panicked expression.

"Oh Brick, thank heavens you've arrived! I thought I'd surely die at the hands of your arch enemy, the space pirate, Dark Kang!"

"Cut!"

The room was flooded with lights and a short bald man smoking a cigar strode towards them. "How many times do we hafta go over this, Wilma, its Ming Ki-Khan, Dark Kang is the villain from last week's episode!"

"I'm sorry, Mr. Goldstein, I guess I'm just nervous," the blonde woman said.

Goldstein frowned and threw his hands into the air. "That's it for tonight, we'll wrap up tomorrow at 7 AM sharp. Don't be late or you're fired!"

Kofi Zedi watched as the crew dispersed from the set. He'd recently been hired as a production assistant by Ed Goldstein.

Groans from the cameramen and set workers filled the room as they abandoned their posts with scowls and angry gestures. The smoke started to recede, although the residual meandered across the set-in thin clouds.

The lead actor, Henry Barlow, released the actress, who fell to the floor with a thud. He stormed across the set to catch up with Goldstein.

"Listen here, Ed, this is the umpteenth take we've had to do with this new broad, and she can't get a damn thing right. Can't we just sound edit her line with Darcy's voice?"

Goldstein stopped and turned. Despite the nearly one-foot

difference in their height, Barlow took a step back from the shorter man, who stabbed his right index finger into his chest.

"You listen here, Barlow, if you hadna been screwing around on Darcy to begin with, we wouldn't have had to replace her in the first place. And furthermore, I don't give a rat's ass how big of a star you think you are now or how many contracts you have with the big studios, you owe me the last two episodes of The Adventures of Star Blazer and you better deliver, or else."

Barlow narrowed his gaze. "Or else what?"

"Or else I'll sue your ass," Goldstein said as he pulled the cigar from his mouth and blew smoke into Barlow's face.

"You wouldn't dare." Barlow stammered.

"Wouldn't I? You may be rubbin shoulders with some hotshot Hollywood producers, Golden Boy, but you best remember where you came from and not try ta weasel your way out of our contract."

Barlow's eyes widened at Goldstein's threat before the director turned and walked away. "I'll remember this, Ed! One day I'll be walking amongst the stars, and you'll see. I bet you'll be begging me to play lead in one of your crappy, low budget projects then."

"Kofi!" Barlow yelled.

The tall young black man made his way towards Barlow. "Yes, Mr. Barlow?"

Barlow had peeled off his tunic and thrust it and his helmet at Kofi. "I want you to polish the helmet and personally dry-clean the tunic."

Kofi nodded. "Yes, sir," he said before he walked away.

He had been fifteen years old when he'd met Barlow

almost a decade ago. His father was a tour guide in Tanzania who happened to have led the safari Barlow had commissioned. On that expedition, his father died saving Barlow's life from a group of gem raiders, in search of a fabled stone called the Star Blazer. It was this story which led to the title of the television program and source of Barlow's newfound status.

In return, Barlow had taken Kofi in as his guardian, used him as a valet and hired him out as a set extra from time to time. Recently, Mr. Goldstein saw Kofi's work ethic and decided to make him a permanent production assistant.

Kofi couldn't really complain, he was treated with more respect than Barlow treated his women, but that wasn't saying much. Nonetheless, he had his own dreams of one day being an actor like Harry Belafonte, his cinema idol. He read Barlow's scripts and sometimes acted out his part after everyone else had gone home.

Once he was off the set floor, he made his way to Barlow's dressing room and closed the door. He knew that the show's star would be "busy" with the new girl, Wilma, and he'd be alone. Kofi put on the Star Blazer tunic and decided not to stop there. Kofi switched out his own slacks and shoes for one of Barlow's extras.

Once he was fully garbed as Star Blazer, he stood in front of a full-length mirror and smiled. Of course, he knew the idea of a Negro man starring in a science fiction film was absurd; he was nothing if not a dreamer. Kofi had received training as a child in African sword fighting with the ancient seme swords, so he took the prop attached to the uniform belt and assumed a battle stance.

"You'll never take me alive, alien scum!" he said, taking in his reflection.

Kofi blinked as his image in the mirror appeared to shimmer. He had been working for sixteen hours straight and attributed this mirage to being tired. As he turned to walk away, a bright light flashed in the corner of his eye. Kofi turned back to the mirror, which rippled like water in a pond.

My eyes must be playing tricks on me.

He couldn't believe his eyes and cautiously approached the mirror.

Is this some sort of special effect prop?

The light flashed again from within the mirror's surface. Kofi leapt back with a start, as tendrils of light reached out and grasped him. He struggled to free himself, but to no avail. He started to yell out for help and found himself pulled into the light before he could utter a sound.

THE ANDROMEDA STAR SYSTEM

In the distant future…

Sharp pain assaulted Kofi's head. He tried to move, but found himself frozen in place. He strained with all his might and managed to make his eyelids flutter.

"Hey, he's waking up," a voice shouted.

Kofi opened his eyes to the blurry image of a small green face staring at him. It appeared to be a cat of some sort and it sat on his chest.

"Where am I?"

The cat stared at him with a wide grin for a few more seconds before he yelled, "Guys, he's waking up!"

Kofi knew he had to be dreaming because cats weren't green, they weren't capable of grinning, and more importantly, they couldn't talk.

A warm sensation coursed through his body as his ability to move returned. He reached up to grab the cat off of him.

"Hey, whatta ya doin', ya big ape? Get your stinkin' paws off me!"

Kofi flung the animal away and sat up. The room resembled the set of Star Blazer, only much more colorful and elaborate.

His eyes zeroed in on the cat, and he couldn't believe what he saw. The feline was dressed in a blue jumpsuit, miniature military boots and stood upright like a human. It reared its back and snarled at him. Its front paws were shaped like human hands and held a large scalpel.

"You take it easy there, partner, I don't want things to get any uglier than they already are," the cat stammered.

Kofi's mind raced at what he saw.

How could this be real?

He heard a soft whoosh and movement caught his peripheral vision before he turned. Three people entered the room through an automated door.

"Sacred Shamkaar, the prophecies have come to life!" a lavender skinned woman exclaimed. She was strikingly beautiful, with long dark purple hair tied into a ponytail. She wore a black jumpsuit beneath silver gleaming armor. The hilts of two large swords extended above her shoulders from her back.

Behind her, to the left, stood a hulking humanoid creature

Kofi estimated to be about seven feet tall, bald with dark blue skin and chains wrapped tightly around its massive forearms. He wore a skintight sleeveless red jumpsuit and black boots. His face bore a menacing scowl with glowing opaque silver eyes.

On her right stood a simple humanoid creature with skin that appeared to be hewn from solid granite, smooth gray with flecks of white and black. Its face had no features other than large black eyes and a slit for a mouth. This creature stood nearly a half foot taller than the first, yet was equally as massive.

"What the hell happened to me? Where am I? And who the hell are you folks?"

The woman kneeled with a bowed head. "You have been transported from a time long ago and from a faraway galaxy to fulfill a great destiny. You are in the Andromeda Galaxy; we are the Space Sentinels and you are the Star Blazer."

Deafening silence lingered in the air.

"My name is Kofi Zedi. Star Blazer is a character on a television program."

The lavender skinned female slowly raised her head. She placed her hand on her chest before she spoke. "I am Kala-mura, former princess of Valkaar, on the planet Burkah. The large, blue skinned warrior to my right is Epic, last of the Titans. The green furred mammal to your left is Booster, of Ailuros. And behind me is Petros, the last of an unknown species. You are aboard our starship, the Helios."

"Why did you take me from my planet and bring me here?"

Kalamura looked to the others and back to Kofi. "Every

two thousand years, an anomalous event in the time/space continuum occurs, called the Conflux. We sought to secure and protect the sacred gem. It was prophesized that an ebon skinned stranger from another world would become caretaker of the Star Blazer."

Booster slowly stood to his full one-meter height and approached Kofi. "What the purple princess isn't telling you is that this basically means it's now your job to protect the entire universe from all the forces which threaten it. Of course, we were just gonna chop it up and sell the smaller gems on the black market, but what are ya gonna do?"

Kalamura gave Booster a fierce glare.

"What, you want me to lie to the caretaker?"

Kofi's mind raced. This was like elements of the television program had come true.

A thunderous boom accompanied by the entire room quaking snapped Kofi from his reverie. "What was that?"

Kalamura stood and strode past him to a large control panel and a view screen. A huge space ship appeared, the likes of which Kofi could never have imagined. It resembled a naval ship with large wings like a commercial airplane.

"It's the Sojourn! Gar-Lan and his marauders must be aware that we have the Star Blazer in our possession," Kalamura said.

Booster was next to her reading from a smaller screen in another console. "Our shields are at 65%, another hit like that and we're going to be in trouble."

"He's hailing us," Epic said.

The image of the ship was replaced with that of an odd-looking creature with red scaled skin, large black opaque eyes and tentacles where a mouth should have been. "You merce-naries think that you could swindle Gar-Lan out of one of the most powerful prizes in the universe? Release the primitive life-form to my custody and I might spare your miserable lives. Otherwise, I will surely destroy you!"

Booster hopped onto the console and stared at Gar-Lan and pointed at him with his humanlike fore finger. "Uh, if you destroy our ship, then you destroy the Star Blazer too, you moron!"

A few moments of silence lingered before Gar-Lan responded. "Prepare to be boarded."

"And what makes you think we would surrender so easi-ly?" Kalamura asked.

Gar-Lan bellowed with laughter. "Because you have no other choice."

The lights briefly turned off only to be replaced with red auxiliary lighting. Nine shimmers of light appeared in the corner of the room and formed into armored figures about six feet in height and armed with an assortment of futuristic rifles, pistols and swords.

Kofi couldn't believe his eyes, first green talking cats, colorful aliens and space ships, now armored monsters materi-alizing in front of him.

The closest armored figure leveled his rifle at them. "I am Kal-Dak, second to Gar-Lan. You are to surrender the Star Blazer to us or be executed."

Kalamura had drawn both swords and stood in a defensive stance. Epic's eyes glowed as the chains on his forearms constricted, while Petros morphed his hands into large hammer heads. Kofi looked around and couldn't spot Booster.

"Space Sentinels, strike!" Kalamura yelled.

Kofi dove for cover as the melee began.

The invading aliens fired their weapons, which filled the room with bursts of concussive light. Kalamura deflected those fired at her with her whirling blades and plowed forward against her foes. The weapon's fire didn't appear to have much effect on Epic or Petros, who barreled into the armed aliens with their massive bodies.

Something tapped Kofi's shoulder. He turned to see Booster holding two weapons. One was a baton about nine inches in length and the other was a small rifle which he kept for himself.

"Hey Earther, here's your weapon."

Kofi looked quizzically at Booster, "My weapon?"

Booster narrowed his eyes. "Yeah, the sacred energy blade. It comes with the job as caretaker to the Star Blazer."

"But this isn't a sword, it's just a stick."

Booster placed a hand across his face and shook his head. "You really are clueless, aren't you? Try to focus your thoughts into extending the energy blade."

Kofi closed his eyes and concentrated on the weapon in his hands. A surge of energy flowed through him like a current of electricity and a yard of light shot from the end of the weapon.

"Well, I'll be John Brown!" Kofi exclaimed.

Booster looked back at him. "Who the hell is John Brown?"

Kofi smiled. "It's just an expression from my planet."

"You Earthers are really weird," Booster said before he leapt out into the fray. "What are you waiting for, ya big ape, you wanna live forever?"

Kofi's smile widened. He'd dreamt of playing this role on stage, and now he'd play the role for real, as he rose with his energy blade in hand and waded into battle with aliens light years from Earth.

Kofi utilized his training in African sword fighting and applied those techniques to his use of the energy blade to devastating effect. He parried the thrust of an alien sword and spun with a slash which gutted his foe. The elaborate katas helped him to better evade the weapons fire and block oncoming blasts with his energy sword. The weapon seemed to almost have a life of its own, as Kofi wielded it.

The others were more than holding their own against Gar-Lan's minions. However, for each wave that fell, almost twice in number replaced them.

"We can't fight these guys forever; do you have a plan?" Kofi asked Booster.

The emerald feline hissed as he fired his rifle and took out another armored alien. "No, just to survive. Gar-Lan won't rest until he possesses the Star Blazer."

Kofi dodged a blast from one alien's rifle and parried a sword strike from another.

"Get down!" Epic yelled, as he shielded Kofi from the pistol's blast.

Kofi looked up in time to see the blue behemoth snatch the pistol from a marauder's hand and backhand him. The force of the blow sent him flying into the far wall. He slid down the wall to the floor in a crumpled heap.

"Are you injured, Caretaker?" Epic asked.

Kofi looked on, still stunned by his near-death experience.

"No, I'm fine. Thanks."

Flashes of light filled the room as Gar-Lan's armored minions disappeared from the ship.

"Gar-Lan's marauders are retreating," Kalamura said.

All had been transported back to the Sojourn, including the dead.

"Booster, fire up the chrono-engines. We've got to time jump," Kalamura ordered.

Kofi narrowed his gaze at the lavender skinned woman. "Time jump?"

"Yes, we have to leave this area immediately because the only reason Gar-Lan's marauders would be recalled back to their ship is if their leader was dead."

Kofi looked on puzzled. "Dead? Who killed him?"

"I did!"

All eyes turned toward the view screen to see the image of a hooded figure staring back at them.

"Who are you?" Kalamura asked.

The person in the image chuckled before they pulled back the hood to reveal a face disfigured with severe burns and lacerations.

Kofi stared in disbelief. "Mr. Barlow?"

Kalamura looked back at Kofi. "You know this man?"

"Yes, he's Henry Barlow. He was my employer. What are you doing here, and what happened to you?" Kofi asked.

"Henry Barlow is dead. I am Kar-Vaak. Our probe detected the energy signature of the Star Blazer within this primitive life form on an infantile planet called Earth. However, it was mortally injured when its terrain vehicle left the hewn path. Due to the frail physiology of this species, we were forced to imbue its mortal coil with Cosmic Cells in order to revive it. I have utilized its base memories in the service of the Shadow King himself, to retrieve the Star Blazer."

"Oh no," Kalamura said. "Malevolence knows."

Kofi gave her a sidelong glance. "Malevolence? Who is that?"

Booster sighed. "Who's Malevolence? He's like, only the Shadow King, epitome of evil throughout the known galaxies. A cosmic terrorist hell-bent on ruling the universe."

Kofi swallowed hard. "Well, when you put it like that."

"Princess Kalamura, your orders?" Epic asked, from a control console where he was seated.

"Get us out of here now!" Kalamura barked.

Seconds later, Kofi's skin began to prickle with an intense heat, and his vision blurred. The room appeared to stretch on into infinity. It reminded him of the reflection one would see in a Funhouse mirror. Time seemed to stop for a moment before everything around him exploded in a dizzying array of colorful lights and white noise.

Everything came to a standstill. The image of the large spaceship on the view screen had been replaced with multi-colored ribbons streaming past them.

Kofi crumpled to the floor and fought the urge to vomit.

"We did it, we successfully completed the time jump," Kalamura said. "We can stay hidden within the time/space continuum, which should keep us out of Malevolence's sight for a while."

"Why?" Kofi asked.

Kalamura smirked. "So that we can make you worthy of the Star Blazer mantle."

Over the course of several months, which seemed like years, Kofi Zedi endured extensive and grueling physical conditioning. He had always prided himself in keeping in great shape, but nothing could have prepared him for this. The training threatened to literally kill him several times over. Yet, he survived.

Surviving had been something Kofi had grown accustomed to and thrived at. From his time as a youth in the wilds of Tanzania, to the concrete jungle of Los Angeles and the vicious social climate of his planet.

"Kofi Zedi, please step forward," Kalamura said.

Kofi stepped up to the alien princess and stood at attention. He wore the Star Blazer uniform, complete with the energy blade and a particle pistol. The helmet carefully secured under his left arm; he held his clenched fist over his heart.

"You have successfully completed the required training of the Space Sentinel Squadron. You have proved, without any doubt, to be worthy of the title Space Sentinel and to serve as our Captain. Congratulations."

Kofi bowed his head as the other Space Sentinels assembled on the bridge of the ship applauded.

"Thank you, Princess Kalamura," Kofi said with a smile.

Booster sat on a perch near the navigation console. "So, Captain Zedi, what do we do now?"

Kofi smirked. "Oh, I don't know. Booster. Perhaps we'll let the gem choose our course."

The golden jewel once housed in Kofi's tunic had been

retrofitted into the ship's central processing unit and formed a unique, quasi-sentient matrix called Star Blazer.

"Hello Captain Zedi," the baritone voice rang out.

"Star Blazer, select a destination along the time/space continuum. Look for any anomaly worthy of our attention."

"Acknowledged, sir. Initiating coordinates," Star Blazer responded.

In an instant, the Helios and its Space Sentinels crew, led by their new captain, caretaker of the sacred Star Blazer, continued on their journey into the far reaches of space, in search of their next adventure.

Author's Note

Well, you have reached the end of *The Best Is Yet To Come*. The title of this collection is my personal catchphrase. Although not an original creation or concept, it speaks to how I see the future and as a commitment to my readers. As I move forward in my writer's journey, I hope to continue to grow and evolve while entertaining my readers.

Always remember…

THE BEST IS YET TO COME!

John F. Allen is an American writer, began writing stories in the second grade, and pursued most forms of writing throughout his career. He is a member of the Speculative Fiction Guild and the Indiana Writers Center. John studied Liberal arts at IUPUI with a focus in Creative Writing. He served in the United States Air Force and is a current member of the America Legion. John's debut novel, *The God Killers*, was published in the summer of 2013 by Seventh Star Press. John was born and currently resides in Indianapolis, Indiana with his wife Mia.

www.johnfallenauthor.com

johnfallen@johnfallenauthor.com

www.ingramcontent.com/pod-product-compliance
Lightning Source LLC
Chambersburg PA
CBHW070933250626
47159CB00009B/3228